For a moment, Daniel lost himself in the depths of Clara's charcoal-rimmed, gray eyes.

He saw intelligence and humor and a liveliness she kept far too hidden. He was drawn to her, as helpless against the tug as metal drawn to a magnet, and he wanted to see more and more of her. "You have made some excellent observations about the robbery."

A pleased surprise lit her face, and he continued. "I would appreciate hearing your insight into this crime. Your feminine intellect"—her eyes flared at his turn of phrase—"approaches the problem from a different angle."

The glare softened.

He plunged ahead. "Are you willing to meet with me from time to time to discuss my progress in the investigation?"

She studied him, one gloved finger on her pursed lips, as if judging the genuineness of his request. The hand lowered and covered her heart. "I believe you mean it, Captain Tuttle."

He held back a smile and nodded.

She shook her head. "Few men of my acquaintance would ask a woman for advice on a criminal matter." She held out her hand. "It would be my honor, sir."

Honor. The word rang hollow in a heart wanting. . .what, he couldn't bring himself to put into words. He took her hand. "To our joint endeavor. May we find quick success."

Award-winning author and speaker **DARLENE FRANKLIN** recently returned to cowboy country— Oklahoma. The move was prompted by her desire to be close to her son's family; her daughter Jolene has preceded her into glory.

Darlene loves music, needlework, reading, and reality TV. Talia, a lynx point Siamese cat, proudly claims Darlene as her person.

Darlene has published several titles with Barbour Publishing. Visit Darlene's blog at www.darlenefranklin-writes.blogspot.com for information on book giveaways and upcoming titles.

Books by Darlene Franklin

HEARTSONG PRESENTS
HP650—Romanian Rhapsody
HP855—Beacon of Love
HP911—The Prodigal Patriot
HP931—Bridge to Love

Love's Raid

Darlene Franklin

Heartsong Presents

To my newest grandchild and only grandson, Isaiah Jaran. May you live up to your name, to proclaim the truth that the Lord is salvation.

A note from the Author:
I love to hear from my readers! You may correspond with me by writing:

Darlene Franklin
Author Relations
PO Box 721
Uhrichsville, OH 44683

ISBN 978-1-61626-288-4

LOVE'S RAID

one

Maple Notch, Vermont
Wednesday, October 19, 1864

The grocer's wagon flew past Clara Farley as she walked down the road, the wheels spewing dirt and rocks that coated the skirt of the dress she had chosen for this special occasion.

The dust settled on Clara's glasses, and she dug blindly through her reticule, looking for the handkerchief she had tucked away earlier that morning. She rubbed the lenses while listening for approaching travelers. The road between Maple Notch and St. Albans carried a fair amount of traffic, but young Dixon had ridden as if the entire Confederate Cavalry chased him. Clara didn't intend to allow the next passerby to mow her down.

A glance back at the house she shared with her brother reminded Clara she had reached the midpoint to her destination. Either return home for a change of skirt and arrive late, or arrive on time with a dusty habit. She lifted her chin. She had never been late in her life, and she wouldn't start today—not with so much depending on the meeting at the bank. Picking up her skirts, she turned her face to the center of town.

By the time she reached the common ten minutes later, every man in the town center had gathered around the grocer's wagon. Among the mix stood one of the men she was supposed to meet at the bank in five minutes, the town constable, Daniel Tuttle. His brother Simeon, the banker, might be there as well, but Daniel stood head and shoulder taller than anyone else in town. She frowned. Had he forgotten their appointment?

Daniel looked straight at her and smiled, if that pained grimace could be called a smile, and touched the brim of his hat. So he hadn't forgotten their meeting, after all. She relaxed and waited to hear what news had the men so agitated.

Daniel's voice rose above the clamor. "If you'll all be quiet, Mr. Dixon will explain what happened this morning." He didn't speak louder. He didn't need to. He exuded the kind of confidence and control every successful schoolteacher mastered. If she could do half as well with her prospective students, she'd consider herself well ahead.

The men in the circle quieted down, and Dixon climbed back on the wagon.

"I had gone to St. Albans to make my usual deliveries like I do every Wednesday." Dixon allowed himself a self-satisfied smile at the mention of his marketing of Widow Lawson's fine, sharp cheese.

"T'weren't cheese that sent you back here quicker 'n a jackrabbit," Brent Frisk joked. "'Sides, it looks like you still have the rounds of cheese there in the back of your wagon." He bent over and lifted one out of the bed as if to prove the truth of his statement. "So explain yourself."

Dixon's face blanched, and he looked at his feet. Clara inched forward, as eager as the gathered men to hear the news. Then his usual bonhomie reasserted itself, and he said in his best orator's voice, "Them Confederates have taken charge of St. Albans and robbed all their banks!"

Gasps echoed around the circle, obscuring anything else Dixon said.

"Them Rebs! All the way up here in Vermont?"

The question froze Clara to the core. Had the war, subject of many heated debates at Middlebury Female Seminary, arrived on her doorstep? It wasn't possible. She had spent hours tearing bandages, had read the accounts of Dorothea Dix and Clara Barton nursing on the battlefield, listened to her roommate Savannah's pining for her southern beau, mourned with pretty Miss Trudeau's grief when her fiancé had died at Gettysburg. But never, ever, had the war invaded Vermont until today. St. Albans was only a short ride away. She put her hand to her throat, checking that the top button was secure.

The men looked like they were ready to go to their homes, grab the nearest weapon, and race to St. Albans. These men, most of them unwilling or unable to go to a distant war, would fight like the old Green Mountain Boys militia when one of their own was threatened.

None of the men gathered had fought in this war and returned to tell about it—none except Daniel Tuttle, the newly appointed town constable. Her eyes sought him out. His right arm had clamped on to the stump of his left arm, as if by holding it tight he could hold in all the memories and feelings brought about by that war. His face darkened, but when he lifted his head moments later, his hazel eyes blazed. While the men continued throwing out suggestions, Daniel carried on a quiet conversation with Dixon. He nodded a couple of times before calling a halt to the hubbub around him.

"Looks like I'll have to earn my pay sooner than you expected." Daniel's lips lifted in a half smile. "Dixon thinks the folks of St. Albans fought back. I'm asking for a couple of deputies to ride with me and check out the situation."

Every man's hand shot into the air.

"I appreciate your willingness. Frisk, Gamble, you come with me. Dixon is in charge of gathering our local militia. Someone needs to stay close in case Johnny Reb decides to head our way next."

All around Clara, men straightened their shoulders.

"I'll send word once we've ascertained what's happened." Daniel jumped on the back of his horse faster than most men with the use of two arms, and the three men turned in Clara's direction. He paused in front of her. "I'm sorry to put off our business, Miss Farley."

Clara had almost forgotten her business with the Tuttles in the excitement of the announcement of battle at her doorstep. "Another time. Godspeed, Mr. Tuttle."

He touched the brim of his hat and kicked his horse into a gallop down the road past her farm.

❧

Men going into battle said they conjured up an image of the woman from back home whenever they wanted to remember there was life and beauty and reason after the ugliness of war.

Daniel Tuttle didn't have a sweetheart, but if he did, he bet she would have dark auburn hair and ridiculous glasses that hid the beauty of eyes as gray as Clara Farley's. He knew the color, because he had spent enough time staring at her when they contested each other for every spelling bee at school. The change in her when he'd come home from the war had surprised him. But then, he had changed as well.

They had crossed the bridge heading into St. Albans when Daniel pulled up his horse. So far, no sign of any traffic ahead, nothing to mar this sunny autumn day with a hint of winter's chill in the air. "I'd better tell you what little I know. Dixon said there were two dozen of them rebels, more or less. One of them jumped on the steps of the hotel and shouted, 'This city is now in the possession of the Confederates States of America!' The soldiers herded everybody onto the town green. He said he was never so afraid in his life."

"So how'd he get away?"

"Dumb Rebs. They couldn't figure out if they were fighting a war or robbing a bank. As soon as they had their loot, they skedaddled out of there. Dixon headed back to Maple Notch to let us know."

Gamble scrunched up his face. "Do you think they'll take us for more of them Rebs?"

"Not likely." Daniel resisted the urge to scratch the stump, his constant reminder of the war. He grabbed his once-blue forage cap from his pocket and pulled it on his head. "We've all done business in St. Albans a time or two." He draped his rifle across his saddle horn and leaned forward. "Ready?"

Frisk and Gamble nodded, and the three of them took a slower pace as they approached town. They passed the still-smoldering remains of a burned-out woodshed. Daniel tightened his grip on his emotions. He didn't see any flames ahead, and no soot cloud darkened the sky. Perhaps this fire had no connection to the events of the day.

A group had gathered in front of one house, one that

rivaled his grandparents' home for size and importance, and he recognized the home of Governor J. Gregory Smith. The governor was supposed to be in Montpelier this week, according to the paper. If he was at home...

Daniel sped up his horse.

"Halt!" A uniformed guard stopped him before he could approach the crowd. Daniel relaxed his face, making sure they could see the badge on his chest and the color of his cap.

"That's all right, Jones." A man dressed in the uniform of General Custer's cavalry strode up the path—the governor's brother, if Daniel remembered correctly. "Captain Tuttle, sir. Has the news of our little contretemps here this morning reached Maple Notch already?"

"Our grocer came to town making a delivery when the—incident—happened."

"Ah, yes. I remember seeing Dixon's wagon."

"We came to find out the true facts of the affair—and to learn if our militia could assist in hunting down the rebels."

Smith pushed his cap back on his head. "They've already hightailed back over the border to Canada, and we can't get to 'em there." He snorted in disgust. "They managed to make off with more than two hundred thousand dollars, and they killed a man and burnt down a woodshed, but that's all. Not much more than a skirmish."

Daniel doubted the folks of St. Albans would feel the same way, but after the battles the two soldiers had seen, he knew what Smith meant. "Send one of your men straightaway if they come back."

"The same to you." Smith turned his glare to the north, the direction where the rebels had fled. "I hope today isn't a portent of things to come—little bee stings up here in the north to distract the battles going on down south."

"Yes, sir." Daniel couldn't agree more. He had come home to escape the ravages of war, to heal, to recover his confidence, if he were honest with himself.

How could a man fight an enemy when he was missing half an arm?

❧

After all the heated comments of the men gathered on the common, Daniel half expected to meet them racing down the road to St. Albans when he returned. But they stood in a straight line, Dixon inspecting their weapons and making notes on his grocers' pad. Every now and then, he motioned for his assistant to bring him something lacking in the man's kit. The group had doubled in size. Daniel spotted Clara's brother, Lewis, among the additions.

One of the Whitson twins noticed them first. He ran to his horse, his rump in the saddle before Daniel could open his mouth. "Where's the action?"

The gathering stilled with his shout.

Daniel waited until he reached the group on the common. "There isn't any."

"Are you saying they didn't rob the banks this morning?" Whitson demanded.

"I know what I saw." Dixon sounded tired, as if he had repeated his story countless times throughout the day.

"They escaped back to Canada, and we can't cross the border to chase them." Weariness washed over Daniel. This job was supposed to allow him time to recover, not demand he head back into battle. He longed to slip from his horse, eat a bite of supper, and relax, but the safety of Maple Notch came first.

What else? "They may come back and strike somewhere else next time. Be on the lookout for any strangers in town. We think the Rebs up in St. Albans came in two or three at a time. We'll post an extra guard by the bank, and we'll also patrol the roads leading into town." Roads left the town common in four directions: the one he had traveled that day, which meandered north to St. Albans; the one past his family's farm, going south to Burlington; the one heading east to Jeffersonville; and the one going west to Fairfax. He named the families and men responsible for patrolling each path.

The men scattered, talking amongst themselves. Only Frisk, Simeon, and a handful of others remained, the ones with homes and farms along the Old Bridge Road. They settled who would patrol the road that night, and the others left Simeon and Daniel alone.

"I'll look into hiring an extra guard for security at the bank." Simeon clutched the lapels of his coat close as the wind picked up and swirled leaves in their direction. "Although I've had trouble finding good men who aren't already working."

"I'll come by more often." Daniel swallowed a yawn.

Simeon peered into his brother's eyes. "Come home with me for a bite to eat. My Molly will have plenty fixed."

Daniel appreciated the offer and the good intentions he knew lay behind it. But he refused—not for the first time.

"Not this evening. I will come on Sunday, as usual. No, a simple dinner and a good night's rest are all I need." He managed a thin smile. "We can expect Miss Farley to present herself bright and early tomorrow."

Simeon's gaze wandered to the east side of the common, where their grandparents' house stood. "If she has her way, you will be our guest, like it or not, before too much longer."

Daniel shrugged. He'd seek a room in town if the house sold. How could he explain the desperate need for solitude that quieted his soul and restored his spirit, which needed healing as much as—nay, more than—his arm?

Which was why he'd just as soon Clara Farley did *not* get her wish to buy the Bailey Mansion.

But he didn't say any of that to his brother. Instead, he tipped his cap and said, "See you in the morning, then."

❧

Thursday, October 20, 1864

At least the day's delay had given Clara the opportunity to brush the mud splattered on her skirt. They were still in mourning. Papa's death only a few weeks after her graduation from the seminary still shocked her. God had blessed her with the will and training to be independent and strong. She needed it.

She paused in front of the door to Lewis's bedroom and lifted her hand to knock. No, she decided. He had been up late, patrolling the road to St. Albans, perhaps the most important route of all since it led straight through St. Albans and on into Canada. Even through the closed door, she could hear his loud snore. At least he had taken responsibility for the patrol.

Don't be so uncharitable, she scolded herself. A good four years younger than she was, he was hardly more than a boy pushed into the position of titular head of the family far too soon. In an unusual move, Papa had made her guardian of Lewis's portion of their inheritance until he reached his twenty-fifth birthday.

She descended the stairs and headed for the kitchen. After the delay in meeting with the Tuttle brothers yesterday, she had expected nerves to overtake her this morning, but she felt quite the opposite. Perhaps the trouble in St. Albans had put her dreams into perspective.

Or perhaps it was the memory of the solid confidence that oozed from Daniel Tuttle. He made her feel safe, and she was certain he would be fair. His brother Simeon, while a good man, was a banker and the grandson of a banker, and had about as much charm as most bankers she knew. In other words, like a caterpillar crawling across a leaf.

Wind rattled the windows, and she hoped Lewis would think to chop up some more firewood before cold weather settled in for the long haul. After she finished the dishes and set aside two muffins with jam on a plate for him when he awakened, she checked her appearance one last time in the hall mirror. The deprivations of war and her wire-framed glasses had done nothing to soften her pinched face. Her thick, not-quite-auburn hair was her one vanity, and she refused to feel bad about it. For this business occasion, she pulled it back in a bun and covered it with a dark brown hairnet. She dressed simply. The craze for hoops puzzled her. What sensible woman would want her ease of movement restricted so by a contraption wider than most doors? She had bought one hooped dress for her graduation and didn't even wear it then, due to her father's ill health. Today she settled for a flowing skirt that would allow her to check out each and every room of the Bailey Mansion for its suitability as a girls' school.

At least she hoped she could check out the house that day. No one expected the eldest Tuttle brother, Hiram, to take a break from his farm as the harvest season drew to a close. Daniel might well be following up on yesterday's events. She sighed at the thought of facing Simeon alone, afraid his banker's face would put an end to all of her hopes and dreams.

She stopped by Lewis's room one last time on the way out. Groans issued from within, and she tapped on the door. "I've left you breakfast on the table." She took his mutterings as an acknowledgment and headed out.

At least today no one raced past her as she walked into town. She did run into Jericho Jones patrolling the road. He reined in his horse when he spotted her. "Where are you headed this fine morning, Miss Farley?"

"I have business in town."

Jericho frowned. "Can't it wait? We're encouraging people to stay close to home until we know those Rebels have disappeared for good."

Clara lifted her chin. "I'm not afraid. I have business in town that won't wait." She relaxed her posture. She knew she appeared haughty when she stiffened up like that. "Besides, I'm sure I'm perfectly safe with you and the other fine gentlemen of Maple Notch patrolling the roads."

He smiled his acknowledgment. "Nonetheless, I'll come back by, to check that no harm comes to you."

"Thank you, Mr. Jones." She didn't want to offend him. Enough talk circulated around town already about her progressive views. What had ever possessed her to ask at a ladies' meeting what was so terrible about women getting the vote, after all?

The crisp air encouraged a brisk walk, and she took quick, firm steps, noting spots where she would stop on the way home to look for leaves. Ever since childhood she had loved collecting leaves, but arriving at a business meeting with a bag of damp mulch wouldn't convey the impression she wished to create. If all proceeded as she hoped, she might indulge herself on the way home.

She only caught sight of Jericho Jones' figure one more time before she reached the town green. Somewhat relieved not to see the militia gathered in the center, she walked past the church building, down the west side of the square, to Bailey's Bank. Baruch Whitson stood straight and motionless as an iron post by the door. She looked up the long length of him and blinked. He reminded her a little of the guards she had heard about at the palace where the Queen of England lived.

"Mr. Whitson? Are you keeping all our valuables safe today?"

"As far as it's in my power, ma'am, yes." He winked at her, and she relaxed. His solemnity the moment before had frightened her. He opened the door, and she walked in, only to discover long lines of people had arrived before her.

Ahead of her, she saw a former schoolmate, Margaret Beacham, her reticule held tight in her hands. "Margaret? What's the cause for all the business this morning?"

Lines crawled over Margaret's forehead as she wrinkled

her face. "Didn't you hear what happened yesterday, how those awful Rebels robbed the banks in St. Albans?"

Before Clara could answer, Margaret continued, "Of course you did. That's why you're here. To get your money before those Confederates rob us all blind. It's what any sensible person would do."

Clara froze. All her money, every penny left to her by her parents except for the house and its furnishings, lay in an account in this bank.

What would she do if it was robbed?

two

Clara breathed in, counted to ten, then slowly released her breath. "That won't happen. Forewarned is forearmed, they say, and everyone is taking precautions against an attack here. Why, there's even an extra guard outside."

"What good is one armed guard against a platoon? They tried to burn down Governor Smith's home yesterday." If possible, Margaret's eyes widened even farther. "What if they try to burn down the bank, with us inside it?" She looked ready to bolt.

"If they do that, they can't get the money." Clara had seen this kind of hysteria before, when the prediction that "this war will be over by Christmas" had proved untrue. Once again, unnecessary fear stood ready to grab people by their throats, this time in her hometown.

"That's true." Margaret bobbed her head and inched forward in line.

Clara looked for Simeon Tuttle in his office but discovered him deep in conversation with the older Dixon, one of the wealthiest men in town. Given the crush of people at the bank today, she didn't expect he'd have time to see her. Her shoulders slumped. How long must her dream take second place behind more important matters?

A hand tapped her shoulder, and she jumped. She whirled around and found herself face-to-face with Daniel Tuttle.

"I'm sorry. I didn't mean to startle you."

Her hand flew to her mouth, and she pulled it away. "I was gathering wool, I'm afraid." She refused to look like a scatterbrained woman in front of this man. "I was hoping we could meet today to discuss our business, but your brother has his hands full this morning."

Daniel's eyes swept the crowd. Clara had the feeling he knew not only the names and ages of every person present, but also the number, make, and model of every weapon brought into the bank. He brought his gaze back to Clara's face. "Give me half an hour. I'll meet you at the house. I would offer you a seat in our waiting room, but. . ."

"It's already occupied." Three more people had come in behind Clara while she was talking with Daniel. Pastor Beaton, who had come to the church after she left for the women's seminary, almost bumped into her. "Are you waiting in line, Miss Farley?" At her response in the negative, he swept forward to take her place behind Margaret.

Stymied by yet another delay to her business with the Tuttles, Clara considered stopping by the café for a cup of tea and a slice of toast while she waited. The establishment had closed for the day, as had Dixon's Mercantile and every other business in town except for the bank. The air was turning cold, so Clara went to the one place she was certain would have open doors—the church.

The building had changed some over the years. The elders had even considered enticing Richard Upjohn to design a new building. Clara was glad the congregation had decided against it. Comfortable pews had replaced backless benches, and an organ accompanied music once sung a cappella. A bell tower replaced the old steeple. Yet for all the changes, she felt a peace, knowing that people had come here to meet with God ever since the town was first established in 1763.

Her hand ran over the plates indicating who had donated money for which pew: in loving memory of Stephen Reid. . . Hiram Bailey. . .Solomon Tuttle. . .James Dixon. Founding fathers, all. The newest and shiniest one read In Loving Memory of Albert L. Farley. Her eyes welled. "Oh, Papa, I miss you so!"

She sat down in the pew marked with her father's name and said a prayer that she had made the right decision regarding her inheritance. Lewis wasn't entirely convinced of the wisdom of her plan.

But every time she asked the Lord, she received the same answer—peace. Straightening her shoulders, she picked up her reticule and headed out the door.

ða.

"Keep an eye out for trouble." Daniel spoke so only Whitson could hear. "I don't like the looks of that crowd."

"Yes, sir. Do you want me to stay inside the bank?"

Daniel considered the idea but shook his head. "Simeon will let you know if he wants you inside. Until then, I need you out here, keeping an eye on any trouble coming from the outside. At least no strangers have shown their faces in town today."

"Not that I've seen. You can count on me, Captain." Whitson's eyes gleamed, almost as if he wished some action would come his way.

"I'll be over at the Bailey House if you need to find me." Daniel shook off the feeling of unease that settled on him like a swarm of black flies in June and instead focused on his upcoming meeting with Clara Farley. "Go ahead and lease it. Sell it, if she'll take it." That was Simeon's advice when Daniel had sought him out a few minutes earlier. "With the run on the bank today, we could use the funds."

But Daniel didn't want to stay inside for any length of time, not until things returned to normal. A quick run through, that's all he would allow Miss Farley today.

As he thought of her, she stepped out of the shadow of the church and into the sunshine. The autumn light shown on her dark chestnut hair and bounced off the sheen of her unrelieved black clothing. In spite of her severe hairstyle, modest style of dress, and those ridiculous spectacles, she couldn't hide her beauty. He kept his smile inside. She wouldn't want him saying so. From what he remembered of the dark-haired beauty, she'd keep discussion on a strictly business level. She would never use feminine wiles to gain an advantage. . .and was convinced she had no wiles to try in any case.

A fine mind and a sharp tongue, that described Clara Farley well enough. The day suddenly seemed more pleasing as he crossed the common, rubbing his hands in anticipation of the lively discussion he would have with the young miss. He lengthened his strides to make sure he arrived a few steps before she did.

"I hope I have not kept you waiting." Her soft voice didn't fool him, not when he knew her sharp eyes had marked his progress across the common.

"Not at all. I'm sorry I had to ask you to wait." He extracted a key from his pocket and opened the door. Grandfather

Bailey was one of the few people in Maple Notch who bothered with locked doors. After the troubles yesterday, the precaution no longer seemed so strange.

How cold and quiet the house seemed, even though Daniel lived there now. The staircase gleamed as much as ever, and sun poured through the windows as it always had, but without the laughter of children, the smell of his grandfather's pipe, Cook's delicacies baking in the kitchen. . . what life was left in the house had died along with his mother.

If Clara noticed his hesitation, she didn't show it. "I've never been upstairs." She set her right foot on the first step and paused to look up the wide sweep of the staircase.

"Grandfather liked to do everything on a grand scale." He smiled at her as he offered her his right arm.

She accepted without even glancing at the place where his left arm should be and ascended the stairs. "I was thinking the treads here are wide enough to allow numbers of people to move at a time. They're not narrow and restrictive, like some I've seen."

His hand tingled where their arms were linked. Upon reaching the second floor, she studied the stairs continuing on to the nurseries. "I'll check there later."

Clara went to the room at the front of the house. "This must have been your grandparents' bedroom."

He nodded. "Simeon removed a few pieces, but we will rent the rest furnished, if you like."

She scrunched her face and pulled a folding ruler from her pocket. "I think the space might be better used as a classroom. Do you mind?" She handed him the end of the ruler and gestured at the wall. Bemused, he watched her unfold it, then run it the length and breadth of the room, marking down numbers in a little notebook. She stuck the pencil behind her right ear and measured the windows next. She couldn't quite reach the top of the window pane, so he lifted his long arm and held the ruler for her. His eyes fell on the notebook, where he saw a rough sketch that approximated the layout of the room.

"I didn't realize you had studied architectural drawing."

She peered at him over the top of her glasses. "What, this? We studied room arrangement at the seminary, how to make the most of. . ." She paused in midsentence. "But you don't want to know all of that. Let me see the other bedrooms on this floor, please."

So there was a proper way to decorate a room? His lips curled at the thought. His mother had known how to make a house a home. Whether the small cabin she had lived in at the beginning of her marriage—now dubbed the newlyweds' cabin by the family—or the Bailey house, she had placed her own stamp on it. He reached down and lifted a pot with dried lilacs in it and felt her spirit in the empty spaces of the room.

Unlike Simeon's wife. Molly owned many beautiful things but could never make them coordinate. Clara could, he was certain of it. He'd have to find an excuse to visit the Farleys' home one day.

Clara made her way to his mother's room next. Daniel hesitated at the door. He knew that the writing desk still held the paper and quills she had used to write letters to his father during their secret courtship, when his Aunt Peggy had acted as a go-between. Once again, out came the folding ruler and notebook, neat figures and drawings added on its pages.

Did the woman intend to measure every room in the house? He thought about the old servants' quarters on the third floor. No one had been up there since he'd returned home, and cobwebs and who knew what else had collected over time. That decided him.

"I promised Simeon I would come back to the bank quickly. Things are too unsettled for me to spend much time on personal business." He stretched his lips in what his youngest sister insisted was a dazzling smile. "Perhaps we can arrange another time next week, when we are more certain if Maple Notch will be affected?"

She opened her mouth then closed it and smiled. . .her own version of a polite smile to match his. "I had my heart set on seeing the house this week. I will be here at ten o'clock tomorrow morning. Of course, if those Confederates do make another showing, I will reschedule."

He found himself agreeing to her suggestion. He escorted her outside to the corner where the road to her home ran, glad to see Jericho Jones patrolling the road. "Any sign of danger?"

"Not a thing. I've ridden down as far as the bridge to St. Albans, and you wouldn't know there'd been so much as a gun fired yesterday." He nodded at Clara.

"You should be safe heading home, Miss Farley."

She graced Jones with a genuine smile, not the polite version Daniel had seen earlier. "I'm certain of it, Mr. Jones. The Lord is paving my way with sunshine." She gestured to the sun directly overhead. "I intend to enjoy every minute of this beautiful weather for as long as it lasts." Picking up the edges of her skirt, she set off at a brisk pace.

She didn't look back to catch Daniel watching her when she stopped to examine scarlet maple leaves where they had fallen to the ground. When her posture relaxed, she looked beautiful—demure, even. A woman like that was open to life and love.

Daniel found himself glad that he had arranged another meeting with Miss Farley.

❧

Clara had chosen a sensible violet gingham for today's meeting. After wearing the same outfit for two days, she decided she wanted a change of dress. A restless night had turned into a restless morning. So taken up was her mind with today's meeting with the Tuttles, she'd had trouble focusing during her quiet time. Prayers for a positive resolution to their business mixed together with an occasional guilty prayer for the people of St. Albans and others fighting far away.

Lewis was already in the kitchen when she came down. He looked her up and down, and she felt heat rushing into her cheeks. "What has you up so early?" she asked, more to divert his attention from her appearance than because she wanted to know.

"The lads and I want to check out a bit of business." He grinned his cocky smirk. "We could use some extra income if your plans go through." He looked at her again and smiled. "Looking as good as you do today, I'm sure you'll succeed." He poured himself a cup of coffee.

The strong scent of the hot beverage wafted across her

nostrils. "I'll take a cup of that, if you please."

"It's strong." He poured her a cup.

"I know. The stuff you make always is. That's what I need this morning." She rubbed her eyes, yawned, and took a sip. No stronger than she expected, but still she frowned and shivered.

"Cream? sugar?" Lewis stirred some more into his cup.

"No. It doesn't make it any more. . .palatable." She slathered a slice of bread with honey butter. Sweets called for a strong beverage, like coffee. "Do you want a hot breakfast?"

"No." He grabbed an apple from the barrel. "Don't wait supper on me either. We may be gone overnight."

"What are you up to? Who are you going with?"

"Oh, the usual group. Bradford, Dupre, Ford."

He hadn't told her everything, but he was a man. She couldn't treat him like a child reporting to his parents. "Godspeed then, brother."

He leaned over and kissed her cheek. "I'll take that as good luck."

Lewis wasn't big on faith, one of her major prayer concerns alongside the war and her school. From the window, she watched him strap a satchel behind him on his favorite horse, Shadow. The dappled gray matched his impulsive temperament, while the silvery white Misty suited her far better.

What business did he have in mind? In the wake of Wednesday's attack and yesterday's panic at the bank, she was glad someone had found reason for hope. *I'll take that as a sign of things to come.* She smiled at the thought. After she put away the breakfast things, she draped her coat about her and started down the road to town.

Cold snapped in the air, but the sky remained cloud-free. Before long, they would have the first snow of the season, but this was perfect weather for walking. Jones passed her on the way into town. His posture had relaxed since yesterday; he no longer peered into the trees, ready to jump at shadows.

Before she arrived at the town common, she saw Daniel riding in her direction. When he reached her, he dismounted. "Simeon wants to meet with us first to review your financial information."

Clara's heart skipped. That sounded promising. "Certainly. I have the information right here."

She expected Daniel to climb back on the horse, but instead he ambled beside her. They walked in silence for a short time. She was about to ask for news from St. Albans when he said, "I love walking through the woods in the autumn. 'Tis one of the things I missed."

Clara's travels were limited to a school trip to Seneca Falls to discuss the importance of the 1848 convention about women's rights. She would enjoy the opportunity to travel more. . .but not under the circumstances that had dragged Daniel away from home.

"Not that I missed our winters. They would have made camp life miserable." He chuckled.

"You can laugh about it?"

The amused sound stopped. "There was a camaraderie among the men, a sense of purpose, much as my grandfather must have felt when fighting for independence. That, and the music. There's nothing like music to ready men for battle."

"I am thankful for your service. Slavery has been a blight

on this country ever since the beginning. If our Founding Fathers had taken a bolder stand then, there wouldn't have been a need for this war. For your sacrifice." She touched him on the shoulder above the arm that ended at the elbow. He jerked away.

"It is what it is."

They had reached the common. Daniel tethered his horse in front of the bank and led her inside. A few customers milled about doing business, but with none of the panic she had observed yesterday. Pastor Beaton stood at one of the windows, perhaps rethinking whatever business he had conducted yesterday. She hoped people would reopen their accounts for the Tuttles' sake. For the town's sake. A town needed a strong bank.

Daniel directed Clara to Simeon's office. As soon as he saw them, Simeon stood and bowed in Clara's direction. "Welcome, Miss Farley. Please take a seat. Would you like a cup of coffee? Tea?"

Clara cleared her throat. "Perhaps a glass of water?" Her throat might not manage the discussion otherwise.

Simeon motioned a clerk nearby and told him what was needed. Daniel settled in the other chair, drumming the fingers of his right hand on its arm. Clara felt his eyes studying her, a grin at his brother's antics lurking behind those light brown eyes.

"Study your opponent for signs of their mood before speaking." Miss Featherton's words on conducting business came to Clara. *"Often you can gain more ground by taking a side path than by a direct approach."*

Daniel's posture told Clara this meeting was Simeon's

show. Whatever reservations and opinions he might have about the lease didn't factor into Simeon's work with the numbers.

As for his brother? She couldn't read Simeon Tuttle as easily, aside from the treatment offered a favored customer. Perhaps he was glad that someone, anyone, wanted to do business in Maple Notch after yesterday's run on the bank. His eyes wandered to the cigar box on his desk. If she had been a man, he might have offered her one. Perhaps she could ask if she could take one home to Lewis; he would enjoy it. The thought brought a smile to her lips, but she refrained from making the request. She would best serve her interests with him by displaying her fine grasp of finances, as Miss Featherton had so often encouraged.

She dug her folder out of her carrying case and placed it on his desk. "I have brought an accounting of my finances, as well as my business plan, along with me today."

"How well prepared you are." A smile flitted across Simeon's face. "I have the record of your account at the bank in front of me." He laid the two documents side by side for comparison. Daniel slipped behind him and bent over his brother's back, a slim shadow of Simeon's more rotund figure. Clara expected Simeon to raise questions, but Daniel spoke first.

"I see there is a monthly stipend drawn on the account in your brother's name. A generous amount, by all accounts."

Clara felt a slight heat pulse in her cheeks. "My father began the practice, and I decided to continue it."

"But he is otherwise provided for? He has no claim on the estate?"

Anger raised the heat level on her face. "The disposition of my father's estate is none of your concern. I assure you that the money in the account under my name belongs to me."

"I didn't mean to imply otherwise."

Simeon looked up at the sharp tone in the exchange between the two of them. He smiled with his usual good humor. "We here at Bailey Bank have always appreciated the confidence your family has shown in our humble institution. I hope we can continue to do business together for years to come." A serious expression replaced his smile. "Please tell me more about your plans for a school. Is there truly enough demand that you believe a seminary here in Maple Notch will fare as well as the one you attended in Middlebury?"

Clara took a deep breath before answering. While the subject of education for women and the broader aspects of women's suffrage enflamed her heart, she didn't want to frighten the good men of Maple Notch with her progressive ideas. "I believe women need to prepare as fully for our place in society as men do. After primary school, our options are limited." She took a page from the folder and pushed it across the desk at him. "Here is my estimate of growth, starting with a small class in January. I expect full enrollment within ten years' time."

"Ten years?" Daniel's interruption ridiculed the idea. "In a decade, you will most likely be married, with a home and children to care for. What will happen to your school then?"

Clara counted under her breath before answering. "My business plan allows for additional personnel as the student body grows. Even if I am married with a dozen children, I expect to continue my involvement with the school." *Read my plan before you condemn me.*

Simeon looked up from the document. "She does appear to have laid a solid foundation for the school."

Daniel grasped the paper and ran his finger down the page without taking time to read it properly. "It still is a risk."

"All business contains an amount of risk," Simeon said.

Clara wondered if she should sequester herself from the brothers' quarrel or argue her point. She bit her lip. The words on paper expressed them as clearly as she could out loud. If she spoke, her emotions would carry her away. . .and she might lose her chance. She stared out the window, at the dust obscuring the common as surely as her doubts clouded her judgment.

Daniel saw the dust at the same time. "A posse of horses is headed straight this way!"

Gunfire cracked in the lobby.

three

Daniel had his hand on the door leading to the lobby when it opened from the other side. A man much Daniel's size, but with a complete set of limbs and his face partially covered with a bandanna, grabbed Simeon by the arms. As he often did, Daniel reached with both arms, forgetting his left arm ended at the elbow, and the effort threw him off balance. When he stumbled, a second robber came up behind Daniel and removed the pistol from his holster, twisting his one good arm behind him before leading them out like condemned prisoners.

Gangly Pastor Beaton opened and shut his mouth. A third robber, an identical triplet to the other two in size and build, pointed to the bag in his hand. He went down the line, gesturing for each person to place their valuables inside.

"Are you Confederates?" Beaton asked. For answer, the robber pointed to his jacket. Daniel caught sight of a red rectangle; it looked like a Dixie flag, marked with a dark blue X and thirteen white stars. The jacket wasn't part of any official uniform, but Daniel had seen soldiers on both sides of the line with little by way of official regalia.

Watch, observe—find a way to chase these men down. Daniel's left arm ached with uselessness. If he had two good arms, why, he'd throw the man holding him onto the ground, grab his rifle, and change the situation in a heartbeat.

The man beside him prodded Simeon to his feet and pointed to the safe. Simeon looked at Daniel under his dark eyebrows, begging for—what? A miracle? A whole man for a brother instead of the weakling who had returned? Daniel twisted, but his captor tightened his grip.

While Simeon turned the lock on the safe, Daniel checked out the safety of everyone else in the lobby. A white-faced Clara stood beside the only other woman present in the bank at the hour, Myra Johnson, the bank's one female employee. A fourth robber crowded the male customers over beside the women. Although visibly shaken, no one appeared injured. So who had exchanged gunshots? Had anyone been wounded? Not one of the Confederates, unless he lay bleeding outside. Baruch Whitson?

A chill that had nothing to do with the October weather passed over Daniel. He twisted again, harder this time, but his captor steadied the barrel of a Colt revolver, muzzle still hot and rich with gunpowder, against his temple. Daniel ceased his movement.

The first robber returned with Simeon, a bag heavy with cash and coins in his free hand. Simeon's face had taken on a pale shade of green. It would serve the robbers right if he vomited all over their shoes. Or it might stir their anger, and they might take it out on the nearest target. His brother. Daniel's stomach clenched at his helplessness. What he wouldn't give for two good arms.

The man holding Simeon took his keys and tossed them to a Confederate before tying him up. The other robber went into the office and found an extra set of keys. Meanwhile, Daniel's legs were being tied together by his captor so he couldn't run. Then the man secured Daniel's arms, as well. Satisfied at last, the robber joined the others, who left by the back door, one man keeping his weapon trained on their prisoners until they all exited. Before anyone moved, they heard the click of the key in the door and the pounding of hooves into the dirt.

To Daniel's surprise, Beaton moved first, coming to Daniel's side and untying the knots as simply as he would a pair of shoes. "Are you all right?" The preacher helped Daniel to his feet.

Daniel shrugged. "You take care of the others here. I have to go after them." He reached to his belt loop for a set of keys he kept hidden.

Whitson sat on the ground next to the door, hands, feet, and mouth bound, blood trickling from a wound to his shoulder. Daniel dropped down beside him. "No one was supposed to be hurt."

"No one told the robbers that." Whitson half smiled. "You go after them. It's a clean wound. I can wait."

Daniel hesitated. The robbers had taken his pistol with them, so he'd have to go to the jailhouse for a weapon. The mare that he had left tethered to the railing before his meeting with Simeon and Clara—that seemed so long ago—had disappeared. Sweeping his gaze around the square, he spotted no other horses. They must have been frightened or led away. A fifth member of the gang? He'd lose more time going to the livery after he had his weapon.

"I'll see about a horse. And then I'll take care of Mr. Whitson." Clara's quiet voice spoke from behind him. "You go on ahead."

❧

Clara had followed Daniel outside. Had he realized one important clue the robbers had given away? He must have. She wouldn't waste his time now discussing it.

She had seen Daniel look around for his horse seconds after she had, and after speaking to him, she took off down the west road, where the livery sat a short distance from the common. Mack Jenson was forking fresh hay into the troughs for the animals when she reached the stables.

"Mr. Jenson. The constable has need of your three fastest horses."

"What's happened to his'n? Is she lame?" Jenson laid the hay fork down.

Clara didn't want to start the rumors flying, but it couldn't be helped. "No. A gang robbed the Bailey Bank just now. They took all the horses." When Jenson raised his eyebrow, she added, "I'm getting another mount for him and his deputies while he gets his guns. Hurry!"

"Too bad he can't have Lightning. Already rented him out last night to a customer intent on some serious revelry down in Burlington." Jenson blew out his cheeks and tapped a pair of tongs on each stall door as he passed. He paused in front of a stall that housed a palomino. "Spotty here's the next best." He continued down the line, picking out two more. "I'm surprised I didn't hear anything. I was shoeing horses a little earlier. Maybe it drowned out the noise." He wiped the back of his hand on his face, revealing a pale white patch. "Wait. Was that a gunshot I heard?"

"I'm sure they'll publish the details later." Clara didn't want to get caught up in a round of twenty questions with the livery owner. She hurried to get the saddle Jenson indicated for the last horse.

Halfway around the common, she met Daniel with Isaiah Dixon and the pastor by his side. "You got extra horses. Good." Daniel looked at the road beneath their feet. "Too much traffic passes this way for me to tell which direction they went."

"They didn't come by the store. I would have heard them," Dixon said.

"Mr. Jenson doesn't think they went by the livery," Clara said, "but he can't be sure."

"So they didn't go east or west, which leaves north and south." Daniel took one set of reins from her and swung onto Spotty's back, while the other two men mounted their horses. "We'll start with the north road and check for signs they've left the traveled path. They're not going to waltz into St. Albans."

"So you think they're the same men who robbed the banks in St. Albans?"

Daniel's face hardened. Clara almost bit her tongue. "Do you have another idea?"

She shook her head. "Just a possibility. We can talk about it later if you don't find them."

"I'll hold you to it. I don't want you going home until we've checked the north road." His fiery eyes held hers for a moment; then he dug his knees into the horse's side and they galloped away.

"He just told me to stay in town," Clara said under her breath. She blasted out her frustration between her teeth. "And I won't get to look at the Bailey Mansion today, either."

She glanced at the sky. "If I believed more in signs, I would think You were telling me that the school was a bad idea."

So Daniel didn't want her going home along the road to St. Albans. His suggestion should rile her feathers, but instead, she felt warm and cozy, like a chick under its mother's wings. What should she do instead? She checked her reticule and found a few loose coins, enough for a bowl of soup and cornbread with a glass of milk at Fannie's Café. What would she do if Daniel hadn't returned by the evening? Her lips curved at the thought. She would have to head home before the sun deserted the sky, whether or not the constable had returned to town.

But as early as it was, Daniel still might find quick success, and she wouldn't need to spend her money on lunch, after all. A bird called from overhead and landed on the roof of the church. "That's a good place to wait." She walked through the always-open doors and took a seat beneath one of the windows.

I could have been killed! Fears she had been holding at bay rushed in, and she shivered inside her warm cloak. "Take ahold of yourself, Clara Farley." She forced herself to speak clearly, stopping the chattering of her teeth. "Nothing happened to you."

But it had. The consequences of the robbery crashed home. *The bank was robbed.*

All my money was in the bank.

She stared at the empty cross high on the wall behind the pulpit. "Does that mean I've lost all my money? Everything Father left to provide for us?"

She sank to the kneeling rack in front of her. Somewhere

a door opened, but she didn't stir. If she looked like a pious woman at prayer, no one would bother her. Only she and God knew the truth: She couldn't tear her thoughts away from the empty bank vault. The palette of her future, so recently as full of color as the forests in fall, was now as stark and relentless as bare trees in winter. She sniffled.

"Miss Farley? Is that you?"

Daniel Tuttle. She didn't want him to guess the cause of her dismay, not until she thought of a way out of her predicament. She sucked in her breath, dabbed a discreet handkerchief to her cheeks, and stood to her feet.

"Mr. Tuttle. Back so soon?"

"We followed the road into St. Albans and didn't catch sign the robbers passed that way. A winter storm met us on our way back." He pointed to the darkening windows. "Let me escort you home before the road becomes impassable."

She had gone about in bigger storms than this, but she nodded her acquiescence. "I'd best get home. Lewis will become worried about me if I am out in a storm."

"Do you wish to ride?" Daniel gestured to Spotty. Clara looked up at the horse's head, tall even for a horse, and full of spirit. "I'd rather walk, thank you."

Amusement lit his eyes, but he didn't say anything. "I'll lead him, then, and ride him back. Don't want to get caught in the storm myself."

Outside the church, the temperature had dropped, and wind howled through the trees on the common, stripping them of the few leaves left on the branches. She tugged the hood of her cape around her head and tightened the strings.

Daniel waited until she finished pulling on her gloves

before he began walking to the northwest corner of the common, which headed toward St. Albans. "At least the wind is at our back. We won't be fighting it."

The wind did push her forward, speeding her steps. They walked in silence until they passed the building where the Widow Landry took in laundry, the last dwelling in the town proper. Snow sifted from the skies as they reached the open road. Daniel said, "I'd like to hear your theory about the robbers."

So he remembered. First she had a question to ask. "Did you hear them say anything?"

Individual snowflakes landed on his forehead as he scowled in concentration. After a long moment's thought, he said, "No."

"Neither did I."

"You think there was a reason for that? They didn't want to give away their status as Confederates by their accents?"

She shook her head and then realized he probably couldn't see her in the swirling snow. "I don't think that's it. From what I heard about St. Albans, they claimed the town for the Confederacy quite boldly."

He murmured his agreement.

"I'm afraid it's something else."

He paused midstride and turned her to him. "Go ahead. Spit it out."

"What if they didn't say anything because. . .we'd recognize their voices?"

four

Clara waited for Daniel's answer, but he was already shaking off her suggestion. "We *saw* them. We'd have known them."

Her lips thinned into a straight line. "They all wore much the same clothes, and not more than two inches difference in height stood between them. With hats and bandannas hiding most of their faces, we couldn't see any facial features or hair. I don't think I'd recognize my own brother in that getup. Would you?"

He started walking again, and she hurried to catch up. When she opened her mouth to speak, he lifted a finger to his lips for silence, his brows creased in thought. Maybe he was like Papa that way; he would consider facts presented to him before making a decision. They strode along for several yards, the horse following docilely behind them.

At last Daniel broke the silence. "That makes my job easier. . .and harder."

The faraway look in his eyes didn't invite confidences, so she didn't comment. The brisk pace he set generated warmth as they plodded ahead through snow that began to stick to patches of ground away from the road. She hoped Lewis had decided to come home early after all, not staying out late as he'd expected. A light in the window and warmth in the house would be most welcome.

When they climbed the last rise before her farm and she

saw that the house remained unlit and unwelcoming, Clara suppressed a sigh.

"No one's home?"

She shook her head, and he frowned.

"I hate to think of you out here alone with those robbers about."

"No one will hurt me." She had learned how to present a brave front from her days as an assistant teacher with Miss Featherton at Middlebury.

Daniel insisted on seeing her to the front door.

"Do you want to come in for a quick cup of hot tea?"

"I've got a long ways to go before I sleep." Daniel tipped his hat, and she could see that the storm had done nothing to dim the fire in his eyes. "Thank you for the offer."

She shut the door behind her and shivered, whether from the banked fire or from the absence of both Daniel and Lewis, she couldn't tell.

❧

Daniel climbed onto Spotty's back and spared a moment to stare at the dark, lonely cottage. He wished he could whisk Clara away to a cozy fireside with the blink of an eye, some place where she could be waited on and warmed instead of having to do the work of two people. That brother of hers never had been much good. Off gallivanting today, no doubt. *I hope he's stuck somewhere cold and unpleasant.* Daniel shook the thought off as soon as it occurred to him. Lewis might be no good, but he was all Clara had since her father's death. Imagine his life without his brothers Hiram or Simeon.

He clucked, and the horse started moving, head bowed into the wind. Daniel debated walking instead—it would keep him warmer—but decided against it. Better to cover the distance in less time.

Thinking of Hiram, Daniel remembered that his brother had invited him to the family farm today, with news of the progress regarding their grandparents' house. Snow stuck to the brim of Daniel's hat. Hiram wouldn't be surprised if he didn't come in this weather. Daniel had asked his nearest neighbor to deliver the news about the bank robbery. With dark falling fast, Daniel would spend the night at the Bailey house in solitude, the way he liked it.

The way he had always liked it. So why did the image of a certain auburn beauty measuring the parlor now intrude on his thoughts? Two lonely hearts—that was all. Snowy winter nights called for cozy couples in front of warm fires. He straightened his shoulders and encouraged Spotty to move faster.

He might paint a pretty picture, but such was not for him. Would never be for him.

No one would want a one-armed man who couldn't even defend his own bank.

❧

Daniel didn't make it to see Hiram on Saturday either. In the morning, he opened shutters to a world bristling with ice, although the remains of last year's grass showed where a dog's footprint had padded down the snow. A bright sun shone overhead, but that didn't guarantee warming weather. He cranked the window open and stuck his head out—cold enough to burn his tongue.

Shutting the window, Daniel felt his heart pounding, readying his body and spirit for the coming hunt. Times like this he could almost *feel* the blood flowing down his left arm into the fingers of his left hand. How could his body deceive him so? He growled at the stump as if it held the answers.

As his usual penance, he shaved his chin with cold water, as if he could force his body to accept the truth by shocking it into reality. Sometimes he added a cold breakfast to his punishment, but not today. Common sense said to warm the body and carry as much warmth as possible with him into the biting cold.

A few minutes later, he had coffee going in a pot—black mud, Simeon called it, but that was the way he'd drunk it in the army, and that was the only way he knew how to make it. Next he started oatmeal cooking, adding a dash of maple syrup into the mix. Sugar heated up a body almost better than any warm drink. He'd learned those lessons the hard way, around low campfires while wearing the thinnest of uniforms.

He slipped biscuits into the oven. Bacon? Yes. He fried up enough for breakfast and lunch and then forced himself to sit still long enough to eat between big gulps of coffee. Only after he emptied the pan of oatmeal and prepared bacon biscuits for lunch did he head to the closet where he stored his winter gear. He fingered the warm wool of his greatcoat. It would hang loose on him now, but worse than that, the left arm dangled where a hand was expected to appear at the cuff. He might let it go except wind would whistle up the emptiness like a chimney vent, freezing his chest along the way. He dug a jar of safety pins from the desk in the study and did his usual awkward job of pinning with one hand.

At last he could leave. Maybe he could borrow one of Hiram's horses, as soon as he could head out in that direction, and return Spotty to the livery. He kept hoping the robbers would release their horses and that his mare would return home.

Dixon had arrived at the jail ahead of him. "Figured you'd need me today. I doubt many people will make it to the store. My wife gave me a proper scolding for going out."

Daniel smiled. Dixon's wife was one of the sweetest souls in Maple Notch. If anybody wanted to feel better, they just went to the mercantile and sat down with a cup of tea and conversation with Mrs. Dixon.

Unlike the opinionated, vocal, *particular* Miss Farley. The reminder of her theory stirred uneasily within him.

"I heard an interesting idea about the robbery last night."

"From Miss Farley, I suppose."

Daniel cocked an eyebrow.

"Don't look so surprised. I know you took her home last night, and she has an opinion on everything." Dixon sounded like he didn't often agree with Clara's ideas.

"Is there something wrong with that?" Daniel took out his Remington, checking the cylinder and the action.

"Well, Captain, I mean no offense. It's just that she has opinions about things best left to the menfolk." Dixon ran his finger along his mustache. "I guess that's what comes from growing up in an all-male household. Mr. Farley treated the girl as if she were his oldest son."

"Anybody can tell God gave her a sharp brain. I'm sure He intends for her to use it." Daniel put the pistol down with more force than he intended. "This latest notion of hers does make sense. Those men yesterday didn't look like any rebels I ever encountered."

"Of course not. They wanted to blend in."

"Then why sew a Dixie flag on your jacket? Clara—Miss Farley—thinks they could be locals. And I'm thinking she's right."

"Impossible!" Dixon's eyes grew as wide as the penny candy he sold at his store.

"Hear me out." Daniel laid out Clara's reasons for thinking the criminals were local.

"I suppose she handed you the names of the suspects while she was at it?"

Daniel acknowledged the jab with a half smile. "No, she was as blinded as the rest of us because these may be people we know. They could even be people we like. People we've gone to church with."

Dixon slumped back in the chair. "There was a time around these parts that if you were looking for trouble, you'd head over to Whitson's farm straightaway."

Daniel waved that away. "I've heard the stories, too, but that's all in the past. Young Baruch is as sound a man as there is. He even got injured defending the bank."

"He's got four brothers."

Daniel glared at Dixon, who lifted his hands in defense. "I'm not pointing fingers. I'm just saying Baruch is the best of the bunch. Not going to be your family—you'd be shooting yourselves in the foot to do that." He grimaced. "Sorry."

Daniel waved it away. "Let's not worry about motive. Pretty soon we'd eliminate everyone in the county because we know them. Let's think about what we observed about them."

"I didn't see them, remember? I can't help."

Someone nudged the door open. "Is this a private meeting, or may I join you?" Pastor Beaton's thin face appeared at the door, and Daniel remembered he had been part of the cavalry before becoming a pastor.

"Come on in. I'm glad you could join us. You were there and might help me remember something I missed."

Beaton took the only remaining chair in the jail and pulled up next to Dixon. "Have you considered the possibility that locals committed the robbery?"

Daniel shot an amused glance at Dixon. "Actually, I have." Honesty compelled him to add, "Miss Farley suggested the idea. What did you notice about the men who were there yesterday? How many of them?"

"Four, maybe more."

Daniel nodded. "All men?"

Dixon raised his eyebrows again, so high that Daniel was afraid they'd creep into his hairline and disappear.

"We don't want to assume anything. If one of them was a woman, that would be another reason not to open their mouths."

Beaton drummed his fingers on the arm of his chair. "I suppose it's possible, but I doubt it. They were too tall." His lips twitched. "Besides, they didn't look like any women I've ever met."

"My thinking, too." Daniel closed his eyes, picturing them in his mind. "They were all right around five-nine, on the tall side for a woman."

"Any chance it could be a family? Them Whitsons have more sons than you can shake a stick at." Dixon addressed his question to Beaton.

Daniel's lips quirked. "And they're tall. That's why we asked Baruch to guard the bank. Figured he'd frighten robbers away."

Beaton shook his head. "They wouldn't shoot their brother."

Daniel wasn't sure about that. Not after fighting in a war that divided families in half as surely as the Revolutionary War had divided Patriots and Tories back in his grandparents' time. "Right now I'm not putting names to paper. I want the best description we can get."

"I can't say who was tallest. They never stood together."

"The one who held me was the biggest." Or did Daniel want to think so, a small ointment to sooth his injured self-esteem? "But not by much."

"Clothes? Of course, they could have changed," Dixon said.

"I didn't take notice," Beaton admitted. "I took my lesson to look beyond the outside all too literally. I saw inside their black souls." Bitterness edged his voice. "God forgive me and help me to forgive them."

"They were dressed like most people around here, farm folk." Daniel's laughter rang hollow. "Between the wide brims of their hats and those bandannas pulled up to the top of their noses, I couldn't see their eyes or their hair."

"That probably means their hair was cut short." Dixon smiled at their surprised expression. "As a haberdasher, I notice where a man's hairline falls below his hat." He held his hand up before them. "Your descriptions could fit half the men of Maple Notch. So they look pretty average." He turned down one finger. "We don't know what their voices sound like, because they didn't speak." He turned down a second finger. "And we certainly don't want to know what they taste like." His middle finger joined the others flat against his palm.

Daniel smothered a laugh. "That leaves smell and touch. The guy who grabbed me had gloves on." He made himself remember the sensation of the leather touching his skin. "Roughened. They've been used a lot. From cowhide, I'd guess." The smell of pungent manure and clean dirt filled his nostrils, and he almost gagged.

"What is it?"

"Cow manure. He hadn't bothered to clean up."

"Did you notice any other odors, any resembling a shaving cream?" Dixon prodded.

Daniel shook his head. "They smelled like they hadn't had their weekly bath for a month."

"That's not entirely true." Eyes closed, Beaton rocked back and forth on his chair. His nostrils twitched as if trying to track down an odor to its source. "Spicy. It reminded me a bit of church, and of a home kitchen at the same time." He opened his eyes. "I smelled an unusual scent, some kind of hair tonic or possibly cologne. It could have been one of the customers, of course. But I smelled it most strongly when the man passed in front of me to take my valuables."

"He didn't come near me. That might explain why I didn't notice it." Daniel worked his tongue over his teeth before turning to Dixon. "Do you sell anything that might smell like that?"

Dixon frowned. "Spices, church, and a kitchen? Are you sure you don't mean one of Mrs. Beaton's Sunday dinners?" At Daniel's glare, he said, "Of course not. But what kind of spices? Shall we repair to the store to smell all the spices I have in stock?"

"So we're looking for a farmer who uses fancy cologne. Great." Daniel snorted. "We might try your test tonight, but let's make use of the sunshine and cover the roads we didn't check out yesterday, starting with the one going east."

❧

"The snow's not so bad." Clara informed Pooches, who gamboled at her feet. "We should have come out long ago."

He barked as if to say, "It's wonderful!" He fell on his back and rolled, matting his golden fur with mud and slush. If the snow were deeper, she might have joined him and made snow angels. But this snowfall was so shallow a blade of grass could still stick through.

Lewis might not have stacked wood by the fireplace before he left, but he had prepared a cord of wood and left it in the woodshed. More remained to finish. Perhaps she could work on it later today. Maybe the exercise would work its wonder on her mind and keep her from worrying about Lewis.

Where was her brother, anyhow? Had he found a warm and dry place to stay when the weather hit? If he didn't come home tonight, she might ask the constable to keep an eye out for him.

After getting wood stacked in the kitchen, Clara went back outdoors to split more firewood. Miss Featherton had believed in exercise for her girls and wanted them to be independent. More than once, Clara had found herself grateful for the practical instruction her professor had included in her preparation for life in the year of our Lord eighteen hundred and sixty-odd.

She grabbed a pair of gloves and settled her feet about a shoulder's breadth apart. She checked the first log for knots. Not finding any, she aimed for a spot slightly off perpendicular. Sliding her hands down the axe, she swung it down with a satisfying *thud*. A chunk fell on the ground, and the scent of wood chips exploded in the air. A few chops later, she was done with that log. The second log went just as quickly. The sun was shining, and her heart singing as it often did when she spent time out of doors. She tied a bandanna around her head to keep hair and sweat out of her eyes. If she kept moving this fast, she wouldn't have to trouble Lewis for some time yet.

What will I do if I've lost all my money? The question refused to leave her alone. She and Lewis already lived simply. They never wanted for anything; they could change their menu to go without meat one day a week and make their clothes last another year. Since her return from seminary, they had taken care of all repairs themselves, although she had hoped to hire help once she started the school. If they didn't have the money for that, she'd find another way. She jutted her chin out. She'd work longer hours—or find a better solution—and Lewis could pitch in more as well. He knew how important the school was to her, to them.

Does he?

Clara chose to ignore the doubts that wanted to creep into her mind. She set the next log on the stump and brought down the ax.

If Lewis doesn't understand, Daniel does.

The thought halted Clara's momentum. Why did she

think that? Daniel seemed to be dragging his feet about selling the house, although he did have a lot of other things going on. She had seen the amused look on his face as she measured the rooms the other day.

Come Monday, she would see the Bailey Mansion, or know the reason why not.

The longer she worked, the slower she moved, and she had to push to finish the last few logs. The ax shuddered against the wood, and she had to swing it an extra time or two to get it to split right. Clouds filled the sky, and she shivered inside her sweat-soaked chemise. A cool breeze blew through the blowsy sleeves of her dress. She hurried to put the ax in its proper place, to stack the wood for easy retrieval before loading the carrier to bring back inside. Only then did she head inside for comfort. She fumbled with starting a fire in the stove and heated water for tea.

☙

Lewis didn't come home Saturday night, but Clara didn't much care. Sunday morning she woke up with a fever and cough and made the rare decision not to go to church that day.

Monday morning dawned, the sun clear and bright. Clara's bout with illness had disappeared except for a minor sniffle. Lewis's continued absence bothered her more. She settled her cape over her shoulders and considered whether to walk or ride into town. As soon as she stuck her nose out the door, she sneezed and decided she should take Misty—or stay home, which she refused to do. *What will Daniel think if he encounters me on horseback?* The question made her smile. The guards remained on patrol, for all the good they had done last Friday. Then again, the robbers might have been apprehended by now, and she hadn't heard the news.

That was the most likely story. Every person in Vermont looked for the Confederates who had stormed into St. Albans last week. By now, everyone must have heard about the Maple Notch robbery as well, whether or not the same gang pulled both jobs. No one could escape detection that long, could they?

Clara had traveled halfway to town when a familiar figure on a familiar horse approached her. Lewis, coming home at last. She nudged her mare into a trot and came alongside him.

He stared at her through bloodshot eyes, and her heart sank. *Oh, Lewis. Not again.* He had taken off like this after Papa's death, but he had promised never to do it again. The greeting on her lips faltered, and she sat in the saddle without saying a word.

"Go ahead. Tell me how despicable I am and how disappointed you are. The trees are ready to hear all about it." His arms swept in a wide arc, and he swayed before wincing with pain. "Why does the sun have to be so bright today?"

The scolding fled from her tongue. She turned her mare to their farm, and Lewis's horse followed. At least Shadow looked well. Wherever Lewis had been, his animal had received proper care.

How Lewis could be drunk on a Monday morning perplexed Clara, since taverns closed on Sundays. Perhaps he had stayed in a private residence that kept spirits on hand. Once at the house, she helped him from the horse. The muscles in her shoulders, still sore from overuse on Saturday, protested, but she could do most anything when she set her mind to it. Once Lewis landed on the ground, he could walk on his own two feet by leaning on her.

Pooches raced to greet Lewis and stood on his hind feet, planting two big paws on his chest. Lewis swayed, and Clara stumbled a bit under the weight. "Down, boy."

Not receiving the enthusiastic greeting he had hoped for, the dog satisfied himself with running around the pair in circles until they hopped into the house. "You stay out, now. That's a good dog." Clara closed the door in his face.

Lewis collapsed into the chair closest to the fireplace and hung his head in his hands. Clara didn't know where to start. Clean clothes? Fresh coffee? Bed?

Coffee, she decided. He couldn't do anything for himself until he sobered some. At school she had heard tales about pouring cold water on someone in an inebriated condition. If the coffee didn't work, she'd try that next.

After she started the coffee, she went out to take care of their horses. The beasts shouldn't suffer because of Lewis's bad choices. Even so, she rushed her normal routine a bit. The coffee had finished brewing when she returned, a good, strong drink like he preferred. She poured a mug half full and brought the coffeepot out to the parlor with her.

Lewis's head had dropped back against the chair cushion and snores and moans alternately emanated from his mouth. Should she let him sleep?

Exhaustion from everything she had done over the past few days swept over her. No! Why should he get to sleep? She shook him, hard, and he blinked at her. "What's up?"

She thrust the coffee cup into his hands. "Here. Drink this."

He took a sip and gagged. "This is stronger than tar. Stronger even than the way I make it."

She glared at him. "It takes strong coffee to combat strong drink."

A tiny grin tugged at his lips, and he drank it down. "Satisfied?" He leaned back in the chair.

"Not so fast. There's plenty more where that came from." She poured him a second cup. "Do you think you can eat anything?"

The green face he turned in her direction gave her the answer she expected. When he finished the second cup, he didn't ask. He held a trembling hand out to Clara, and she filled it again.

He drank it down in one long swallow—maybe the only way he could stomach the taste—and set the mug on a side table. "I refuse to drink another drop. I don't want to have an accident in addition to all the other problems I have. And now"—he stood, locking his knees together—"I will head to my bed."

Clara opened her mouth to speak. Before the words came out, someone knocked at the door.

Daniel.

five

Daniel saw the movement behind the curtains and waited before knocking a second time. When Clara answered the door, she came out on the stoop with him and shut the door behind her. She looked mussed, as if she hadn't bothered to fix her hair that morning, and her cheeks pinked in the sun.

"May I help you with something?"

Her question made him realize he hadn't yet said a word, let alone explained his visit. She looked at him as if she expected him to set a bag of goods for sale on the ground and start hawking his wares. The day-old beard on his chin probably didn't help matters any.

"When you weren't at church yesterday, I was worried." There, he'd said the bald truth. "With all the ruffians running through Vermont these days, I was afraid harm might have come to you."

"As you can see, I'm doing fine." Her face softened. "You've had no luck in finding the miscreants?"

He shook his head. "I've talked with most folks from town, but I haven't caught up with Lewis yet. Is he here?"

Clara's face went still, and her mouth writhed with unspoken words. "He's. . .indisposed at the moment."

A dozen possibilities flew through Daniel's mind, but soon he identified the most likely possibility. "He's drunk."

"No." She dragged the word out. "Not exactly."

Daniel considered his options. "If he's sober, he should be able to answer some questions. And I wanted to speak with you about our business matter, as well." He waited for her answer.

"Very well." She opened the door, and he followed her inside the vacant room. "He mentioned going upstairs to rest. I will ask him to come down." She grabbed a shirt lying on the floor and headed upstairs.

Daniel hadn't visited the Farley home before. Old Mr. Farley must have mounted the rack of 10-point antlers, fashioned into a hat rack. The rather yellowed antimacassars protecting the chair backs might have been made by Mrs. Farley, long deceased. A dozen things pointed to Lewis's presence in the home. A pipe rack, the muddied floor where his feet had rested, a faint odor of spirits. For signs of Clara, he had to look to the bookshelf, where a Bible rested with a ribbon marking her place, and stationery tucked away for her next letter.

All in all, it was a comfortable, lived-in room, but not a room decorated with the intention of receiving company. What would she do if given free rein in the Bailey house? Would she allow it to run into this state of comfortable disarray, or would she keep it spotless for her students?

He decided he wouldn't mention the subject to Simeon. His wife kept their house like a museum. Of the two, he preferred Clara's approach. He shook his head. He was thinking as if the house already had passed into her hands. That was the problem. He wanted her to have the house so he could see her frequently.

The real reason behind his trip today had little to do

with Lewis and more to do with seeking out the contrary Miss Farley. Back at the jail, Dixon had drafted a chart for the men of the town, tracking what they knew about their movements on the morning of the robbery. Lewis's was one of several blanks left, and Daniel had decided to start the day with him. He hoped Lewis could make a good accounting of his day, for Clara's sake, if nothing else.

Clara returned to the parlor. "He'll be down presently. Would you like something to drink? Coffee? Tea?"

He spotted the coffeepot on the side table. "I'll take a cup of that, if there's any left. I can get it myself." He grabbed a mug from its rack over the table and lifted the pot.

"Oh, but it's terrible coffee. Thicker than March mud." The panic on her face made him want to laugh.

"That's just the way I like it. How did you know?" He lifted the cup to his lips. "Perfect. It takes considerable talent to make coffee like this." The chuckle that escaped her warmed him deep inside.

"At least let me get you a piece of lemon cake, lest you think coffee sludge is the extent of my culinary talents." She didn't wait for an answer but went into the kitchen and returned with a three-inch slab that made his mouth water to look at it.

The cake melted on his tongue, its tangy sweetness the perfect complement to the harsh coffee. He forced himself to pause after two bites. "You missed an important announcement at church yesterday."

"I'm sure I missed more than that." She sneezed. "I hate being away from the Lord's house."

"I know you are a customer of the bank. And I also know

you didn't join the general panic and remove your funds on Thursday."

She stilled her hands, their hold tighter than a dead man's grip.

"The robbers cleaned out the money stored in the bank."

"I guessed as much."

The fearful acceptance in her voice tugged at his heart.

"Cheer up." He took another bite of cake and moaned with pleasure. "A bank's assets don't consist simply of cash on hand. Simeon has invested the money wisely and expects a good return for years to come. In other words, he has personally guaranteed the funds of everyone's deposit. It may take a day or two longer than before to access ready cash, but your funds are safe."

She turned her head away and reached into her reticule for a dab of white lace to blot her tears. "Thank you for telling me."

He leaned forward. "Your welfare matters to me." The way she looked at him with those dove gray eyes, he'd have promised to grow wings like a bird and fly to the moon if she asked him to. Another gulp of harsh coffee brought him to reality, and he settled in his chair. "When do you want to reschedule your tour of the house?"

"And the appointment with Simeon. Provided no one else decides to rob the banks of Lamoille County." The twitching of her lips suggested she held back a laugh. "Actually, I was going to go into town today, but. . .something else came up."

"I have a few more people I need to see today. Let's plan on early tomorrow morning, after school starts."

"I'll be there."

He had time to finish the cake and imagine what else she

could cook if she set her mind to it by the time Lewis came downstairs. He had taken time with his appearance, shaving his chin close, brushing his hair back, donning a clean white shirt. He had prepared to conduct business, but so had Daniel. He was a soldier pursuing the enemy—if he could only identify him.

"Well, Captain Tuttle, Clara said you wanted to see me." Lewis took the biggest chair in the room, the one designed to accommodate Mr. Farley's girth, and crossed his arms across his chest.

He must know about the robbery by now. Clara was a witness, after all. But Daniel knew better than to tell a witness something he might not know. "You had a rough weekend." He made it a statement.

"I confess, I did." Red shot through the eyes that so resembled Clara's in color. "To think those rebels could make it all the way up here. I was shocked, and even a little scared." He spread his hands as if in apology. "Perhaps I'm a coward."

Any man who sees the world through the bottom of a bottle is a coward. But Daniel didn't voice the maxim. He had seen too many men seek courage from any source, including liquor, to chastise Lewis. Neither would he let it interrupt his interrogation.

"When did the binge start, Lewis? How long were you drinking?"

The man blinked as if surprised at such a crass question. "Some friends and I went to the tavern on Friday night. We had heard about the robbery, and we didn't want to go back in case the robbers were still around."

"Which friends?"

"The usual."

Daniel wondered if he would have to drag the names out when Lewis continued. "Bob and Rod Whitson. Ned Whimsey. They were with me the whole time."

Daniel thought about Dixon's distrust of the Whitsons. The twins Lewis mentioned had earned a reputation notorious even for their family.

"There were others? Part of the time?"

"I believe there were," Clara said. "He also mentioned Dupre, Ford, and Bradford. Didn't you, Lewis?"

"I don't remember exactly." Lewis waved his hand in front of his face. "Things got blurry after a while."

A small groan directed Daniel's attention to Clara. The details must be difficult for her to hear.

"So when did you get to the tavern? And when did you leave?"

The tale Daniel pulled out of Lewis included a few times and places and names to check, a sordid tale of nearly three days of a drunken spree. Daniel forced himself not to lecture the young man.

"I'll verify the information you've given me. If you think of anything, anything at all, that might lead us to the criminals, please let me know." He couldn't keep quiet, not entirely. "This kind of behavior does no good for anyone involved— least of all yourself." He left before his temper led him astray. No one should treat Clara the way Lewis did.

◆

Clara's conscience pricked her. Lewis might have started drinking on Friday afternoon, as he said. But neither one of them had told Daniel he'd left home before breakfast. He could have done everything exactly as he said—after he had gone with the others to rob the bank.

Foolishness. Lewis wouldn't have robbed the bank, robbing himself in the process. He was often lazy and even thoughtless, but he wouldn't bring terror to innocent people.

With Daniel's departure, all the starch fled from Lewis, and he sprawled in Pa's old chair. "If you sit like that, you'll ruin that beautiful shirt before you've worn it for an hour," Clara said.

"Then I'll have to take it off." Suiting action to word, he started unbuttoning the cuffs.

"Lewis, you can't stay down here *naked*." As a matter of fact, Lewis had often pulled the stunt as a young boy. But he was a man grown, even if his behavior over the weekend called that into question.

"Then I'll go upstairs." He was about halfway down the front of the shirt now. "I want to rest awhile before tonight."

"Tonight?" Visions of Lewis rejoining the lads for another round plagued her.

"Don't worry. I shall be here for supper and in my own bed at a respectable hour." He threw his arms around her in a brotherly hug and kissed her on the cheek. "I know there must be a God, because I don't deserve a sister like you."

With comments like that, how could Clara stay upset with him, even if his theology was wrong? "Chicken and dumplings?" she asked after his departing back.

"My favorite."

Clara's hopes of a brief afternoon nap faded as every step of making the dumplings took longer than usual—starting with chasing the chicken all over the yard. She tasted the broth. It was a tad too salty, but Lewis wouldn't notice. He poured salt onto everything he ate before taking a bite, enough to burn away his taste buds.

When at last the dumplings were bubbling on the stove and applesauce heating in a pan, she settled down in the closest chair and laid her head on the table.

She hadn't counted more than ten sheep before she heard the tread of Lewis's footstep, but by the clock, fifteen minutes had passed. She grabbed crockery from the shelf, set it out, and retrieved a pitcher of milk from the cold cellar.

"Milk?" Lewis sounded as unbelieving as a heathen at a church service. "I'm not six years old, Clara."

She leveled a look at him, and he put his hands in the air in mock surrender. "Very well, I'll drink it. Tonight."

After ladling out the dumplings, she sat down to enjoy the meal with her brother. She didn't say a word about his activities over the weekend. Instead, she asked, "Do you think George McClellan has any chance of being elected president?"

The way Lewis looked at her reminded her that he had few political interests. "I'll make sure I get to the polls and vote. My first time, you know." He flashed a saucy grin in her direction.

She bit her lip at that statement. Would *she* have the right to vote, a right her brother took for granted, anytime within her lifetime? How old would she be? Women in Vermont, herself among them, fought for that privilege even now. But she kept those opinions to herself. She wanted to get Lewis in a good mood.

They bypassed the emancipation amendment—that

seemed obvious to both of them—and instead discussed whether Governor Smith's lieutenant, Paul Dillingham, was the best choice to succeed him.

She had intended to make apple brown betty, Lewis's favorite fall treat, but settled for warm applesauce with a cinnamon stick in it when she ran out of time. If it stayed chilly today, she might heat some apple cider for a going-to-bed drink. Apples were good whatever form she ate them in.

She added gingersnaps to the warm applesauce. Lewis leaned back in his chair. "That was a delicious supper. Just what I needed." His eyes had brightened, only a few red lines sneaking through the corners to indicate the abuse he had put himself through over the weekend. With a clean shirt, shave, and the tired bags under his eyes smoothed out, he looked young, healthy, and whole.

After setting out fresh coffee for them in the parlor, she took a seat opposite Lewis. The time had come to speak her mind.

"I expect you heard that Baruch Whitson was injured during the bank holdup the other day."

His expression darkened. "Do we have to talk about it? I got enough of a grilling from your Captain Tuttle."

Clara bit back the retort that rose in her throat—Daniel wasn't her anything—and shook her head in a gentle denial. "Nothing like that. I just wondered if Mr. Simeon Tuttle would want to hire another guard until Mr. Whitson has recovered. He might hire more guards because of the current situation. I would."

"And you want me to apply?" Lewis scratched his chin.

"You're a good shot. And strong. You'd do a good job." *And maybe a steady job will encourage you to stay away from taverns.*

Light danced in Lewis's eyes, and she could see the idea take hold. "You say he might be looking for more than one guard?"

"Bound to, don't you think?"

"I think I'll check it out." He bounced out of his chair and came over to kiss her on the cheek. The affectionate look he sent her way warmed her straight to the toes. This was the kid brother she knew and loved.

"I'll put in a good word for you with Mr. Tuttle when I meet with him again."

The spark in Lewis's eyes flickered, but he patted her on the shoulder. "A quiet night at home is just what the doctor ordered for tonight, don't you think?" His grin wobbled. "Maybe you can read me some of that Thoreau that you're so fond of."

"A visit to Walden Pond. That sounds delightful." She'd love to lose herself in the simplicity of Walden Pond and not deal with the shenanigans of humankind, which weren't nearly so predictable. Next to the eternal truths revealed in the Bible, Thoreau enthralled her the most.

She dug in the bookshelf for Papa's copy of the original edition and sat down. Pooches draped himself across her feet as she settled down on the horsehair sofa her mother had loved. She felt Mama's presence most powerfully when she sat there, wrapped up in a coverlet Mama had quilted with her own hands. As always, Clara smiled when she read the title page. " 'I do not propose to write an ode to dejection, but to brag as lustily as chanticleer in the morning, standing on his roost, if only to wake my neighbors up.'" A cheerful shout as lusty as a rooster's crow in the morning—that would chase away the problems of the past few days. "We shall have to visit Concord some day."

"You always say that when you start in on Walden." Lewis laughed at her.

She lifted her chin. "I shall go there with my students, at the very least." She turned the page to the first chapter and began reading. " 'When I wrote the following pages, or rather the bulk of them, I lived alone, in the woods, a mile from any neighbor, in a house which I had built myself, on the shore of Walden Pond, in Concord, Massachusetts, and earned my living by the labor of my hands only.'" She spared a glance at Lewis, wondering if this was the best choice of reading material when encouraging her brother to seek steady employment, but she shrugged and lost herself in the beauty of the woods.

The flames burned low while she read. Her voice cracked as she sneezed and coughed, and at last she gave up. Lewis stirred and put fresh logs in the fireplace. "I'll finish up down here."

Times like this, Lewis was so sweet, she could almost forget the worry he had caused her over the weekend.

Almost.

&

" 'Only that day dawns to which we are awake. There is more day to dawn. The sun is but a morning star.'" Daniel closed *Walden* and put it back in its space on Grandpa's shelf. Thoreau alternately enlightened and confused, expanded and enraged. The mental exercises had proved most helpful while Daniel was in the army, helping to keep long hours of boredom at bay. He wondered what Miss Schoolmarm Farley would say if she knew he had carried a slim copy of the book with him in his knapsack, next to his Bible. When a rainstorm washed away his tent and the two books with it, he wasn't sure which he missed more.

He shook his head. He knew better. Thoreau was only a man, with man's words. He doubted people would be reading them two, three, or however many thousands of years from now, the way they did the Word of God as given in the Bible. No man's words could change a life the way God-breathed scripture could and did.

He walked around the house, as he did each night before bed. Should he go down to the jail to see if any news had come in about the robbers? He shook himself. No need. If something happened, Dixon would alert him straightaway. He needed sleep, but as he had been so many nights before battle, he was too restless to do more than doze. Unlike the battlefield, where he could stare at the enemy's campfires, here he battled an invisible and unknown enemy.

As in the war, his enemy was someone close to him, a fight between brothers and neighbors, the bitterest fight of all. He frowned. At least he had proved his two brothers innocent of the crime. Hiram stayed busy night and day at the farm, and besides, he was well short of five-nine. Simeon had been at his side when the robbers came.

Not that Daniel seriously suspected either one of them. But he had vowed to consider every man in the vicinity, be they friend, family, or foe. As constable, he had to act fairly, but his heart heaved a sigh of relief when he could eliminate his cousins and nephews from the suspect list.

About two dozen possibilities remained, three if you counted men a little too old or who didn't quite fit the physical description they had of the robbers. Tomorrow, he would check the alibis they had provided.

Perhaps he should have gone out tonight. He could have spoken with the barkeep who had served Lewis Farley and his cronies. No, best he wait until morning, when the man might be sober, if cross.

Daniel strayed up to the top floor of the house. Opening the door to the nursery, he could almost see shadows of his former self kneeling in front of the toy chest. He had enough toy soldiers for a battalion, and they marched into battle time and again. He recreated the two battles of Fort Ticonderoga. When he could convince Simeon to join him, they took the parts of their father and his friend Tobias, lurking around Burlington during the second war with Britain. As a boy, Daniel had dreamed of the day he would become a soldier like his father and grandfather. He cupped his left elbow with his right hand. Others before him had died. He shouldn't complain about the loss of a limb.

Although, God forgive him, at times he thought he'd be better off dead. God had protected him from himself, and he had survived healthy of body and of mind. But the sooner he got out of this house, designed for family and children, the better off he'd be. He shut bedroom doors to the taunting echoes of childhood laughter before retiring downstairs.

Hiram counseled him to hold on to the house until the day he had a family of his own to fill the rooms. But Daniel knew better. He would never have a family of his own.

six

Early the following morning, Daniel heard someone pounding on the door. Frantic that he had missed a new development regarding the bank robbery, he jumped into his breeches and fumbled into his shirt while racing down the stairs.

Clara Farley waited at the door. One look at his disheveled state, and she glanced overhead, her nose wrinkling up into her glasses. "I'm sorry. I didn't realize it was so early. You did say to come by this morning and. . ."

He became aware of the empty sleeve dangling below his elbow. He hadn't taken the time to pin it up as he usually did. His shirttails dangled below his waist. Stubble covered his cheeks, which was a good thing, because he could feel heat rushing into them. Since she had a brother, she must have seen men before their morning ablutions, but he was nonetheless embarrassed.

Propriety might dictate she remain outside while he dressed more thoroughly, but the gusty wind stirring her hair convinced him otherwise.

"Come in and wait in the parlor while I make myself presentable." Without further pleasantries, he escaped to his bedroom and dressed himself properly. This morning no comb could tame his hair, so he settled for a splash of tonic. That reminded him of the description of the odor Beaton had detected during the robbery. He didn't feel comfortable asking men what kind of hair tonic or cologne they used; he had peeked around their homes when he could and let his nose do the investigating the rest of the time. Nothing had come to light so far.

He returned downstairs to a deserted parlor. From the back of the house, the odor of sizzling bacon grease and stout coffee teased him. As he made his way down the hall, he heard sounds stirring in the kitchen. Clara had unearthed one of Grandmother's aprons, a yellowed pinafore, and was stirring enough scrambled eggs to feed Hiram's family. Bacon nestled on a stack of toast in the center of the table.

"You're fixing breakfast." *Brilliant conversation.*

She turned around so fast that she almost spilled the eggs from the cast-iron skillet. "It was the least I could do, since I arrived at such a terrible hour." Wrapping her hand with the pinafore the way he had seen his mother do hundreds of times, Clara used it as protection against the heat of the coffeepot as she poured him a mug. "I made it extra strong. I believe you said you liked it that way." She wrinkled up her nose in that endearing way of hers, as if she couldn't believe it.

"I do." He blew on it to cool it a tad and then took a deep drink. "Ah. Just right." He gestured at the eggs she spooned into a bowl. "I hope you're planning on eating something with me."

"Don't worry about me. I had breakfast before I left home." She poured tea from a teapot she had steeping and sat down across from him.

She was so thin, it wouldn't hurt her to eat a little more. She needed someone to take care of her. "I insist. I can't eat all this by myself. You must have developed some appetite on your walk into town." Without waiting for her answer, he grabbed a plate from the cupboard and added bacon and buttered toast to a mound of eggs.

She smiled and nibbled on a slice of toast the way he had seen his sisters do when they wanted to be polite. He pretended not to notice, and soon she tucked into the food with a genuine appetite.

As soon as she cleared her plate, she reached for the now-empty bowl and stood to her feet.

"Sit down." Daniel was surprised how much he enjoyed bossing her around. "Keep me company while I finish eating these delicious eggs. I'll clean up later." He smiled at her, and she eased back into the chair.

He couldn't remember the last time he had eaten such a pleasant breakfast. The only thing missing was hot buttered biscuits.

"I didn't even think of biscuits." Clara looked ready to jump from her chair again, and Daniel realized he had spoken aloud. Now he felt heat rushing into his cheeks. Maybe she would blame the color on razor burn.

Daniel swallowed every bite while drinking three cups of coffee and could have eaten the food Clara had consumed if she hadn't already finished it.

She looked so right, so comfortable, in that kitchen, which had intimidated even his mother. The room had been the cook's domain, and few people challenged it. He could get used to sharing breakfast with a woman like this every day. *Stop it*, he reminded himself. No woman would want him, certainly not a woman as fine as Clara. He took care of the dirty dishes and stilled his racing feelings before returning to the business at hand.

"Thank you for that delicious meal." He rubbed his midsection in appreciation. "Where do you want to look first?"

"I'd like to start with the attic rooms." Her fingers fumbled with the apron ties.

"Let me help you." As soon as he reached for the bow, he could have cursed himself. Her two hands were better than his single hand. He stood behind her, breathing in her fresh scent, like gardenias. She seemed to sense his hesitation and leaned back into him, making it easy for him to hold the strings in place with his stump while his right hand picked the knot apart. He managed to untangle the threads, and she lifted the loop over her neck before replacing it on the hook. He looked at her, their eyes only inches apart. "You said you want to see the attic first?" His voice came out like a schoolboy's.

She nodded.

He smiled, hoping to put them both at ease, and moved to the stairway. He'd never seen her in a hoop dress that he could remember. He didn't know how women managed with those things, although Dixon said they sold almost faster than he could get them in. She didn't lack the funds, so maybe she found the style silly?

They reached the staircase, and he decided she avoided them because of their impracticality. Hoop skirts called for sweeping staircases, even wider than the ones in this house. He enjoyed watching the sway of her hips as she ascended the steps without the assistance of the rail, not pausing even at the second-floor landing. On the third floor, she peeked into the two smaller side rooms, where the staff had slept, without taking measurements.

A pleasant sigh escaped her lips when she walked into the

nursery. "What a lovely room. You must have many happy memories of this place." She walked straight across the room to the window looking out the back. "From the looks of it, there was once a lovely garden back here."

"My mother's pride and joy. Her interest in growing things is what drew her to my father, back in that horrible Year of No Summer when frost killed the crops."

"I don't know how my parents met. Mama never told me before she died, and then Papa was too sad."

How unfortunate. Daniel knew the history of his family back to the days his great-grandfathers had helped settle Maple Notch at the end of the French and Indian War. "I was sorry to learn of your father's passing. I didn't know him well, but from what I could tell, he was a fine man."

"He was." She bent down to examine the books on a low shelf, and a nostalgic look crossed her face. "I see some old favorites here." A smile erased the earlier pain. She pulled out a book with a cracked leather binding. "Your Bible. Of course." She leafed through it, smiling here and there. "I can tell this has been well used."

"A chapter every morning and night from the time I could read. Grandfather wouldn't let me read anything else until I heard from God."

Continuing her perusal, she giggled. "Weems' *Life of Washington* I might have expected, or Webster's spelling book, but *Love Triumphant* by Abner Reed?"

"I do have two sisters." He managed to keep a straight face. He would never admit to reading the book to discover how to get a girl interested in him. His attempts had failed, in any case. No sweetheart stayed behind when he went off to war.

She lifted a stack of magazines with pages half torn out. "Oh, I read so many of these. They look like they'll fall apart if I handle them, though." She settled them back into their place on the shelf and stood. "This room would make a marvelous studio." She took out the same notebook he had seen before and made notations.

A pang struck Daniel's heart at the thought of dismantling the room that held so many childhood memories, but he chided himself. "Will you want to make changes to the structure?"

She finished making a note before she looked up. "If I buy the house, I might."

"And you plan to turn it into a school? For women?"

She looked at him as if he was slow. They had discussed all this before. "Yes."

His heart beat rapidly. He hated to think of this place that had once been both home and retreat turned into an institution. *Where's your sense of family, of the legacy you've been handed?*

Simeon's voice played in his head. *It's too much house for you by yourself. And the truth is, it's too valuable an asset to let it sit unoccupied and unused.*

If they were in a different part of the country, the house would make an excellent place for recuperating wounded. A lot of houses had been pressed into service that way. But praise God, the only action Maple Notch had seen was the robbery last Friday, and only Whitson had sustained any injury.

Be a good steward. Pass it on to someone who can make use of it. Simeon's advice came back to mind. Ever the businessman, he was also a faithful Christian. Trust him to make a spiritual application out of a business decision.

But Daniel wasn't ready to let go, of either the house or its history. He would also miss the excuse to meet with the opinionated Miss Farley. His desire not to see the house changed warred with his curiosity about what she would do with it.

Clara snapped her notebook shut and turned to him. "I'm ready to see the first floor."

❧

Clara took in every detail of the solid carpentry of the house, the smooth finish of the floor, the quality of wood in the stair rail. Hiram Bailey prepared a fine home for his bride, built with pride and quality, and had kept it equipped with the latest of conveniences. It offered plenteous space and a pleasant learning environment—both important qualities in any institution of learning.

She had peeked into the front rooms on her way to the kitchen that morning. An occasional guest in the Bailey home, she had seen the front parlor on numerous occasions. The only room she had never visited on the first floor was the study. Rumor said Hiram Bailey kept a fine library, and she wanted to see for herself.

One glance at the walls of the room confirmed the rumor. She had only seen so many books in one place at the seminary's library. "May I?" When he nodded approval, she took down a title at random—a bound copy of Thomas Paine's *Common Sense*. The pages showed signs of multiple readings. She put it back on the shelf and ran her fingers along the row until she came to a Bible.

"Be careful," Daniel said.

A chunk from the middle of the Bible fell into her hands. Pencil and pen marks covered the pages. "You should keep this somewhere safe." She put it together again and laid it carefully on the edge of the desk, not attempting to stack it back on the shelf.

"I probably should put it away somewhere, but I enjoy reading my grandfather's thoughts. I still read a chapter morning and evening, like he said. Besides, not many people come in here."

Clara continued skimming the titles, row after row of neatly aligned books alphabetized by the author's last name. At last she came to a shelf with an empty spot among the books, suggesting a volume had been removed. She had reached the place where Thoreau's books would be. She found *Civil Disobedience* and *Slavery in Massachusetts*, but *Walden* was missing.

"I'm reading *Walden* at the moment. You won't find it there."

She felt his hazel eyes burning into the back of her neck.

"I made it my goal to read every one of Grandfather's books." He came alongside her. "Then I might start adding to his collection."

She covered her laugh with a hiccup, but Daniel glanced at her.

"Do you find the thought amusing?"

Her hiccup hadn't convinced him. "Oh, no, not at all. I was just reading *Walden* myself last night. I find parts of his work—unsettling. Thought provoking." Clara's hand dropped from the spine of the book she was touching. "I was smiling at the thought of a verse from Ecclesiastes that my schoolmistress used to quote."

" 'Of making many books there is no end; and much study is a weariness of the flesh.' Ecclesiastes 12:12. It was my favorite verse when I wanted to get out of schoolwork." Daniel smiled as he quoted the verse, peeling years away from his face. "Now I find reading very restful."

"I envy you. Access to all these wonderful books." A quick estimate suggested more than a thousand books lined the shelves, and she hungered to read them all. She turned to face Daniel. "I want to buy the books with the house."

Daniel didn't answer, but rather circled around behind his grandfather's desk and took a seat. From there he exuded power and authority, but she refused to let him intimidate her. She took the seat facing him, inching forward, holding her back ramrod straight.

He placed his right hand on the desk, and Clara caught herself looking for the other one. He didn't appear to notice her rudeness. "So you are interested in purchasing the house." He said it as if engaged in a game of chess, plotting his next move. His normally expressive eyes had darkened, blank as wood.

She wondered what he had in mind. She could only play the game piece she had planned to start with. "Yes. I have an appointment to discuss terms with Mr. Simeon Tuttle when we finish here. I am certain we can reach an equitable arrangement."

A faint smile tugged at his mouth. "What if I said the house is no longer for sale?"

seven

After all the meetings, all Clara's hopes and dreams, did Captain Daniel Tuttle intend to crush her like a bothersome black fly? Good humor fled, replaced by a black veil even darker than her skirt. The *nerve* of the man.

"You should have informed me that the place was not for sale before our business together commenced." She could hear her own voice, stilted, high pitched—vinegar and not honey. She swallowed once, then again. Her mouth felt dryer than the mill pond during a drought. "I have no wish to waste your time any further." She stood and tucked her reticule under her arm, seeking escape before she fell into a thousand pieces.

"Miss Farley—Clara—please sit back down." He came around the desk before she could blink. "I'm sorry I startled you. Let me get you a drink."

He stayed gone long enough for Clara to breathe deeply and regain some degree of composure. Perhaps he was still willing to sell the house. After all, he had only asked "what if?"

He returned with a pitcher of water and two glasses. He poured them each a glass and gestured for her to imbibe while he polished off his own with a long swallow. She surreptitiously swished the first few sips around her mouth, moistening the parched places.

"Let me explain myself better. After further thought, I'm

not ready to let my grandparents' home pass out of the Tuttle family."

She took another sip of water, determined not to let her agitation show.

"But I do agree with Simeon that the house needs to be used for something more than a bachelor's residence. So, what would you think of leasing the property instead?"

Leasing. Her mind raced with the idea. "We would need to agree upon the length of the lease. I won't set up school and then have you change your mind two months later."

"Of course. I don't anticipate needing it. . .any time soon." An indefinable something crossed his face.

"I planned to make changes so that it would be more suitable as a school."

He leaned back. "I want to approve any changes."

Did he plan on watching over her shoulder, ready to take over the reins at the smallest sign of weakness? She looked deep into his eyes and decided no, he didn't. Something else was at work here.

❧

Daniel found himself wishing Clara needed a hundred changes made. Then he would have almost endless excuses for spending time with her. But he sensed she might resent his interference. "I'll ask Simeon to draw up the terms of the lease."

Clara frowned.

"Is that a problem?"

She straightened her back further, if that were possible. "An independent party should draw up the contract. I know of a lawyer in St. Albans. We can consult him. I will need to discuss financial details as well. Will you handle that, or will your brother?"

I will. The words tripped on the tip of Daniel's tongue, but he knew he shouldn't do it alone. "I'll tell Simeon what I've decided, and we'll plan on meeting with him in two days' time."

"Good. I will bring some preliminary requests for changes to the house at that time." She cast her glance at Grandfather's desk, and Daniel wondered if she imagined herself in the massive chair, dealing with recalcitrant students.

No, he doubted she would spend much time confined behind a desk. She would be among her students, encouraging, instructing, ordering when the need arose. He found himself smiling. "I look forward to seeing what you have in mind."

"I mustn't take any more of your time." She stood. "Are you making any progress is finding the robbers? Is there any chance they are those Confederates who robbed the bank at St. Albans?"

Considering the fact she was the one who had first raised the possibility of local involvement, her question surprised him. "From all accounts, no. Those gentlemen hightailed it back to Canada, and the authorities up there won't turn them over. You'd think we were still at war with Britain." He shook himself. "Unfortunately, no one is acting suspiciously."

"Suddenly rich? Spending money like there is no tomorrow?"

They arrived at the front door, and he trapped one side of her cloak between his elbow and chest while helping her drape the other side over her shoulder. Awkward. He couldn't even help a lady into her coat without twice as many steps as a normal man. "I'm a little surprised. It suggests a degree of self-control I wouldn't have expected of these ruffians."

"Consider this." She swirled, her cloak settling in soft folds around her feminine form. "The raid on St. Albans presented the opportunity. But they might have been planning the robbery for a long time."

For a moment, Daniel lost himself in the depths of her charcoal-rimmed, gray eyes. He saw intelligence and humor and a liveliness she kept far too hidden. He was drawn to her, as helpless against the tug as metal drawn to a magnet, and he wanted to see more and more of her. "You have made some excellent observations about the robbery."

A pleased surprise lit her face, and he continued. "I would appreciate hearing your insight into this crime. Your feminine intellect"—her eyes flared at his turn of phrase—"approaches the problem from a different angle."

The glare softened.

He plunged ahead. "Are you willing to meet with me from time to time to discuss my progress in the investigation?"

She studied him, one gloved finger on her pursed lips, as if judging the genuineness of his request. The hand lowered and covered her heart. "I believe you mean it, Captain Tuttle."

He held back a smile and nodded.

She shook her head. "Few men of my acquaintance would ask a woman for advice on a criminal matter." She held out her hand. "It would be my honor, sir."

Honor. The word rang hollow in a heart wanting. . .what, he couldn't bring himself to put into words. He took her hand. "To our joint endeavor. May we find quick success."

❧

Clara wanted to skip around the town green as she left the Bailey Mansion. Daniel's decision to lease the house and not sell it surprised her, but the advantages revealed themselves after a little thought. A lease involved no permanent commitment for either party. She would give her all into setting up the finest girls' school Vermont had ever seen. If it succeeded, she would press the Tuttles for a sale later. If it failed, she would determine what steps to take if and when that happened. Miss Featherton had told her she would always have a spot on the faculty at Middlebury, but Clara desired to stay in Maple Notch. At least until Lewis was settled.

If he is ever settled, a rebellious voice in her head insisted.

But no thoughts of schoolrooms made her legs want to break their steady gait. Daniel Tuttle wanted her help in hunting down the robbers. He valued her intelligence. He said so. And in a society that placed more importance on a woman's looks and command of the wifely arts than on the quality of her mind, she found his invitation refreshing—compelling, even.

Clara couldn't face going straight home to household chores. The coins in her purse would pay for a cup of coffee and one of Fannie's famous cinnamon rolls while Clara sketched changes she'd like made to the Bailey Mansion. Passing the school where she had spent many happy hours as a child, she decided to take another detour. What alterations had been made since her student days? Maybe she could pick up some ideas for the renovation of Bailey Mansion.

She opened the door to a loud clamor. Two boys—adolescents—threw spit wads at each other. About halfway down the aisle, a gaggle of girls giggled over the desks. At the front, the youngest children sat in a semicircle. One of them leaned back in his chair and looked straight at her.

"That old spinster lady is here!" He shouted at the top of his lungs, and the room quieted in an instant. All eyes turned on her, including those of the pastor's wife, Mrs. Beaton. Clara wanted to leave and slam the memories behind her, but a good school mistress always kept her chin up and moved forward.

"Nicholas Whitson!" The usually serene Mrs. Beaton sounded a cat's whisker away from chasing the boy out of the schoolroom with a broom. "Go stand in the corner."

Then she glanced at the clock, and her shoulders sagged. "Children, go ahead and take your lunch break."

Pandemonium broke out again as they all scrambled for their lunch buckets and dashed out the door. Mrs. Beaton rubbed the back of her neck as she walked down the center aisle toward Clara.

"Where is Miss Stone?" Clara asked. The same teacher who had shepherded her through her last few years in Maple Notch still taught the local school, becoming the town's institutional old maid. *Apparently I've been elected to join their ranks.* The blush she had suppressed earlier spread across her cheeks at the thought. At least Daniel saw something of worth in her. She raised her chin.

"She suffered a terrible cough in the night. The Sexton children arrived with the news this morning and begged me to take over school for the day. But as you can see. . ." Mrs. Beaton sighed. "My calling is not to the classroom."

"Let me teach this afternoon, then. Tomorrow, too, if

Miss Stone is still sick." Clara's heart pounded. She was still sniffling, but she felt well enough for school. Teaching usually increased her energy.

"Oh, would you?"

Clara put a hand to her mouth to cover the laugh that bubbled up at the relieved expression on Mrs. Beaton's face. "I'd love to."

"But—" Mrs. Beaton glanced at the corner where Nicholas had his nose plastered against the wall, his fingers tracing patterns on the planks. In a lowered voice, she said, "I'm mortified by what that young scamp said."

Clara waved it away. "I've dealt with worse. Go ahead and leave. I'll take over. And I'll plan on coming back in the morning."

"If you insist." Mrs. Beaton grabbed her satchel like a drowning man finding a piece of floating wood. "I'll bring you a sandwich, so you have some lunch." She scurried out the door.

Clara spared a thought for Lewis as she took a step in Nicholas's direction. Her brother could fix his own lunch if he came home, she decided. She stopped a foot away from the boy. He squirmed and sneaked a glance over his shoulder, dread masking his face.

"Do you have something you wish to say?" She spoke to his back.

"I'm sorry for calling you a spinster, Miss Farley."

"Apology accepted." She didn't blame him for repeating something he heard at home. "I will expect you to treat me with respect this afternoon. Can you do that?"

Back still to her, he nodded.

"Then go outside with the others to eat your lunch. Play in the sunshine. I'll give you some extra time."

He dashed for the door, then paused, smiling at her with a grin missing two front teeth. "Thank you, Miss Farley!" When Mrs. Beaton returned with a sandwich, Clara asked about the morning's lessons. As she suspected, they hadn't accomplished much. After a brief discussion to establish each group's assignments, Mrs. Beaton fled in the direction of the church.

Clara perused the history book the older students had been assigned to read. It could have been the same volume she used as a student, every bit as boring: a list of battles and dates and names of people now dead instead of the living, breathing story of people like the children, who had once laughed and loved. All, or almost all, children in the school had at least one ancestor who had fought in one of America's wars.

She knew at least one family that sent soldiers to every war back to the French and Indian War before Maple Notch was founded. The Tuttles. An idea formed in her mind. This afternoon, after she left the classroom, she would stop by the jail. Daniel Tuttle was the perfect person to teach in her classroom.

⁊⬥

Daniel's weary horse needed no encouragement to head home as dark descended. Another fruitless day spent establishing alibis. All the wives said their husbands had gone out to the fields, but would they know if the men had sneaked away for an hour or two? They might not know, but he doubted the married would run the risk.

Stopping by the jail, he was surprised to find Clara Farley waiting for him. A frisson of pleasure removed the weariness that had settled on his shoulders.

"Constable! I'm so glad to see you." Clara looked up from the note she was writing.

"Miss Farley." He nodded at her and removed his hat. "How may I help you this evening? Have you uncovered the culprits on your own today?"

A confused look sped across her face. "I'm afraid not. I'm here about another matter." She gestured with the paper in her hands. "I'm filling in for Miss Stone at the school, and I'd like your help."

School? The change of subject threw him off balance. "I'm at your service."

"The Tuttle family is one of the founding families of Maple Notch. You told me about your grandparents the other day. Who better to tell the pupils about the history of the United States than someone whose family has seen it from the beginning?"

He still didn't follow. "I don't understand. What do you want me to do?"

She blinked. "Why, tell your family's story, of course. Especially about the wars. I believe a personal touch would bring our history alive to the children."

His insides clenched. He didn't want to talk about his war, ever, and certainly not to children.

She swept on, heedless of his reaction. "Textbooks are full of dates and names and statistics. I want the children to know why we're fighting. And you can do that better than most. I've also asked young Nicholas Whitson to bring in his father."

Daniel snorted. "Whitson?"

"A peace offering of sorts." Her cheeks glowed, but not from cold. The possibility enthused her, transforming her into as lively a lass as any in Maple Notch.

He could no more say no than a fly could escape a spider's web. "When do you need me there?"

"When is it convenient for you?" she countered. "I thought we might breakfast together at Fannie's Café." Her cheeks glowed brighter than before. "To discuss my ideas about the investigations, and a few changes I would like to have made to the house." She spoke so fast her words blurred together. "That way, you could come straight to the school and still be on your way early."

"Is seven too early?" he asked.

❧

The sky had darkened to a deep purple before Clara made it home that evening. She found Lewis in the kitchen, holding canned green beans in one hand and a jar of applesauce in the other. Egg whites coated the counter, and she could smell burnt food from the door.

"Where have you been?" he growled.

"I'll tell you over supper. Go sit down. I'll fix something for us to eat."

Since she still had chicken stock left from Monday's dinner, she could fix a quick vegetable soup and cornbread.

She set the stock to simmering on the stove and added a variety of vegetables as well as a dash of salt and pepper and parsley. After she whipped up the cornbread, she cleaned the counter and scraped the eggs Lewis had burned into the slop bucket. She went to the pantry for a few chunks of ham to drop into the soup. Lewis hadn't taken anything for his lunch. Where had he eaten, then? It didn't matter. He was home tonight, not out drinking again.

Within an hour, she brought food to the table, but Lewis didn't come when called. When she sought him in the parlor, he had closed his eyes and splayed his limbs across the overstuffed chair. She knocked on the door, and he awoke, a startled doe expression in his eyes. Then he sniffed appreciatively. "Smells good."

"Wash your hands before you come sit down." She knew he hated the reminder, but like most men, he was no better than a little boy when it came to table manners. He joined her at the dining table a few minutes later, dressed in his Sunday-go-to-meeting clothes, spiffy, if a bit wrinkled.

"Do you want to return thanks this evening?" She always asked. He always deferred to her.

"I believe I will."

He bowed his head and began so quickly that he had said "Lord God Almighty" before she had closed her mouth.

"I thank Thee for Thy bounteous blessings to us who are so unworthy. For this food, and for the hands that prepared it. And I thank Thee for providing a job. Amen."

Before Clara could process or transition, Lewis said, "I'm famished. Let me have some of that soup."

She brought the tureen to him and ladled out a full bowl. "You have a job?" She kept her hand steady against the expectation of surprise.

"Guess who's the new bank guard?" He pointed to his chest. "Me!" He struck a somber pose but couldn't keep it, his mouth twitching with a smile. "They had me start right away, and they want me back tomorrow."

"Permanent?" Clara's breath caught in her throat. She took the tureen to her own bowl and ladled out a smaller amount.

"At least until Whitson is better." Lewis shrugged. "If I do a good job, Mr. Tuttle said he'll find another job for me at the bank. Maybe as a teller."

Clara blinked at that. "That's wonderful."

"This is delicious!" Lewis almost slurped the soup down in his excitement. She hugged his enthusiasm close to her heart. He hadn't acted this happy since Christmas when he was five years old. The last year their mother was alive. Soon his spoon hit the bottom of the bowl.

"Have some more." She had hardly started hers, but she pushed the tureen in his direction. "Take as much as you like."

First he cleaned the bowl with a chunk of cornbread, and then he ladled more soup to the rim. "So, did you settle your plans with Mr. Daniel today?"

Lewis never asked about her day. If landing a job changed him this much, she wished he had found one sooner.

"He offered to lease me the house."

"I thought you wanted to buy it."

"I did. But this may work just as well."

Lewis took his time with his second bowl of soup. Before his next spoonful, he asked, "You're excited about this. Tell me about it."

Once the floodgates opened, she talked without touching her soup. Lewis not only listened, but he also asked intelligent questions. When she slowed down enough to finish her bowl, she scooted her chair to the corner of the table near his chair and laid the notebook with her rough plans for the school—classrooms, dormers, library, the works. She sighed. "I don't know how many changes to ask for. If I ask too much, he might decide not to let me lease the house at all."

Lewis pushed the bowl away from him and leaned back, an amused gleam in his eye. "I doubt that. If you ask me, Mr. Daniel is interested in you."

Heat she couldn't blame on the now-cooling stove flooded her cheeks. "That's ridiculous."

"I agree. Why should you settle for half a man? Why, even at your age, with your inheritance, you should be able to attract the finest that Vermont has to offer."

"Why, you. . ." Anger pounded into her temples. "I do not intend on 'settling' for any man. And if I was interested, Daniel Tuttle is more of a man than I could ever hope to attract if I was eighteen and beautiful and not. . ." Anger fled her, tears taking its place.

"Oh, sis." Lewis put his arms around her in an awkward hug. "I spoke without thinking. I didn't mean to make you feel bad." He patted her shoulder. "You'll find somebody. I know you will."

Clara sniffled, but she blamed it on the lingering cold. "That's all right. I have every intention of becoming Maple Notch's resident spinster, famous countrywide for her school. That's all I've ever wanted."

Liar, her traitorous heart whispered.

eight

Clara took extra time with her toilette in the morning. She decided to break from wearing mourning, for the sake of the children. That's what she told herself. Nothing spelled gloom quite so loudly as funeral attire, and she wanted her pupils to enjoy their day at school. Lewis's words about Daniel last night had nothing to do with it. Nothing at all.

She chose a spruce green and beige gingham that she'd been told highlighted her eyes, with only a black armband to indicate her continued mourning. But the children didn't explain why she fiddled with her hair. She even pinned hair rats, made from strands she pulled from her brush, under the hair on either side of her head, to give her face a softer, rounder shape. If only she didn't need glasses to see. The thin frames emphasized her straight, pointed nose and hid the depths of her eyes. She slipped a reddish brown hairnet into her satchel, in case her hair fell down, alongside sheet music of her favorite songs. Music and story were her preferred methods to teach America's history, not dull dates and names. She'd let Miss Stone drill that information into them when she returned, if she felt it was important.

She left biscuits and bacon in the warmer oven for Lewis when he woke up. When she had informed him of her morning appointment—with enough blushes to paint the sky pink with sunrise—he pretended not to notice and only said he didn't need to report to work until nine.

She took Misty. Lewis had insisted on it, expressing concern for her safety while traveling in the dark. Had the robbery brought them to this, fearful of their neighbors and jumping at every shadow in the trees? She hoped the hysteria would soon pass.

Violence of any kind made a community uneasy. Maybe that's why she didn't enjoy studying the minutiae of war. Even so, she agreed that freedom—from Britain's tyranny and for the slaves—was something worth fighting for.

What stories would Daniel tell? Would he mention realities best left unshared with children? The older boys, who hoped the current conflict wouldn't end before they could enlist, needed to hear the truth. But not in the schoolroom. Daniel had an ear for a good story. He might stretch the truth upon occasion, but his audience would remember the story all the better for it.

She knew she'd remember every detail. His eyes burned with truth and passion, burrowing his way into her heart, no matter how much she denied it to Lewis.

Even though she arrived at the café early, Daniel was already there to help her down from the saddle. After she tethered the horse to the hitching rail, he turned so she could tuck her left arm in the crook of his right elbow, and they entered the establishment like any couple might. She turned her face aside so that he wouldn't see her telltale blush, but she sneaked glances to take in his appearance. He, too, had taken pains with dressing. His white shirt had been pressed, the left sleeve neatly pinned under his elbow; his breeches looked clean; and his hair, combed and slicked back. He looked better than fine—he almost looked like a man come courting. She shooed that thought away.

"How lovely to see you here today, Captain Tuttle! And Miss Farley, it's been far too long." Fannie, the hostess, seated them near the window, where all comers could see her prize patrons. "How may I serve you today?"

Daniel smiled at being given the place of honor. "I'll have your Lumberjack's Special."

"Two of everything, and I'll heat the syrup for you." Fannie turned to Clara as she poured coffee for Daniel—*not* the dark sludge he made for himself, she noted. "And for you?"

Clara had avoided breakfast at home so she would have an appetite, but the butterflies in her stomach wouldn't welcome greasy fare. "A bowl of oatmeal, with some tea, please." The ham sandwich and apple she had packed for lunch would have to hold her over until supper.

"That's not a very big breakfast." Daniel smiled at her and sipped the coffee. Sighing, he pushed it away. "That wouldn't keep a mosquito awake long enough to suck my blood."

Clara pushed the creamer and sugar at him. "Try these. They cover a multitude of sins, Papa used to say."

"If you call café au lait coffee." But he smiled and stirred in a little of both. "It does improve the taste, even if it doesn't keep me awake." He studied her over the cup, which looked as delicate as a chickadee in his hand. "You look nice today, Miss Farley." The hesitation in his voice belied the warmth in his eyes, as if he couldn't help saying the words.

The compliment left her so flustered she said the first thought that came into her mind. "I thought you might wear your uniform."

What warmth she had spied in his eyes fled, replaced by granite. "The last uniform I was wearing wasn't fit to come home in."

She blanched. His last uniform was the one he wore when a cannonball shattered his arm. In a small voice, she said, "I'm sorry."

"Don't be. I survived. Many less fortunate didn't. I tell myself at least I still have both my legs."

The arrival of their food saved them any further discussion on the subject. He had withdrawn into some angry, lonely place. How could she cheer him? Talk about the robbery, since that was one reason for meeting that day? No, she decided. Not yet. In his present mood, he might take it as an accusation for his lack of progress in the investigation. Nothing she could think of would bring back that spark.

A thought occurred to her and made her smile. If she couldn't cheer him up, she'd give him a different target for his anger. "What do you think would happen if I showed up at the town hall on election day to cast my vote?"

He laid down the fork he was bringing to his mouth. "What did you say?"

"I asked what you would do if I came to the town hall to vote on election day. The election *is* only two weeks away, after all." She looked down at her plate, but she had finished the oatmeal, and her appetite had returned. She gestured Fannie over and asked for more tea and a soft-boiled egg.

When she met Daniel's eyes, she didn't encounter anger, but rather, amusement.

"I do believe you're serious." He smiled.

She tossed her head and felt some of the pins she had

used to tuck her hair into place fall out. "If I teach the class tomorrow, I plan on holding a mock election—and let the girls cast their votes as well as the boys."

His mouth opened and shut again, without a single word passing his lips.

She dabbed at her mouth with her napkin to hide her amusement. "The day will come when women will vote, you know. I hope it's in my lifetime. If not, certainly in my daughter's." She realized she had spoken of a daughter she had no prospect of bearing. Clara could see the girl, a lovely, auburn-haired beauty with fiery hazel eyes that lit up like the sun. Heat scorched her cheeks.

❧

Fannie returned with the requested food, and Daniel took advantage of the time Clara spent cutting the top of her egg off to drink his coffee.

Within seconds, Fannie arrived to refill his cup then went off to serve other patrons. He frowned at the pale brown surface. Too much coffee in the cup to make café au lait. Instead, he drank from his glass of water. "I suppose you plan on teaching these radical ideas in that school of yours." His smile stretched wider.

Clara look so stricken, so worried, that he hastened to put her mind at rest. "Don't worry. I won't hold it against you. In fact, people might pay good money to see you give a speech on the subject."

"It's not a laughing matter." She lifted her chin in that way that said she wouldn't listen to any arguments.

"Who's laughing? I think I'm on to something here. Make Maple Notch the greatest learning center in all of Vermont.

All of New England, for that matter. Why limit our horizons to those young ladies you hope to bring here? Why not enlighten young men as well?"

When he saw the thoughtful look cross Clara's face, he regretted the words he'd uttered in jest. She sat straight in her chair, spoon poised over her eggcup, eyes alight with some inner thought process. When she came to life again, she shook her head and took a bite. "What you propose is an intriguing idea. Someday, perhaps, but for now, I am happy to further educational opportunities for young ladies." She put down her spoon and looked at him. "I apologize for my earlier question about your uniform."

He stiffened, and she must have noticed. She hastened to add. "I was thoughtlessly thinking of the classroom like a stage, and what props an actor might bring. That's not quite what I mean. I hope you understand." She dropped her gaze again.

He took her hand in his. "Look at me." In the depths of her eyes, he saw a mirror of the anguish he allowed himself to feel on his worst days. "I know you didn't mean to offend."

She sipped her water then moistened her lips with her tongue. "You don't have to discuss your own experiences in the war unless you want to. I have no desire to bring back unpleasant memories."

He rubbed the back of her hand with his thumb. "Don't worry. There are some good memories. I can mention friends and training and campfires and belief in God." He could fill hours in the classroom without mentioning the smells of decay, the frigid cold and the stifling heat, the metallic taste of blood in his mouth, the horror of the surgeon's knife. . . . He trembled.

Now she held *his* hand. "It might be best not to mention your part in the current conflict at all. Some of the students are...overeager, shall we say. I'm afraid they would pester you with questions."

He regained his equanimity. "Then all the more reason I should tell them something. They all know I fought in the war, and if I don't mention it, they may ask me questions I don't care to answer."

He had been there from the beginning with the Army of the Potomac, from its first skirmish during the Peninsula campaign back in '62 through the horror that was Gettysburg, when General Sedgwick issued his famous order, "Put the Vermonters ahead and keep the column well closed up." When they covered the draft riots in New York, Daniel began to think he might survive the war unscathed. Then his regiment joined in General Grant's overland campaign, and half their number died or were wounded. Only five months had passed since then. As soon as the surgeons determined Daniel would survive the infection that set in after they amputated his arm, they sent him home. The town rewarded its hero with the position as constable. His mouth twisted. No one had foreseen bank robbery or the Confederate invasion of Vermont.

Clara's hand, a lifeline that kept him from sinking beneath the morass of his memories, withdrew from his grasp, and she reached for her reticule. Then he felt a sheet of paper slip beneath his fingers. He looked down and saw a sketch of the second floor of the Bailey Mansion.

Her lips straightened, eyes bright behind her glasses, she had moved on from discussion of the war. Her businesslike demeanor reminded him of how wrong he was to think of Miss Farley in any terms except that of friendship.

"The second floor would be our dormer floor. I would like to divide the master bedroom into two separate compartments."

Divide up his grandparents' bedroom? *I promised I would consider the changes she wanted.* Maybe he expected suggestions along the lines of extra shelves or furnishings, not structural adaptations. He studied the drawing, but it made about as much sense to him as the maps their captains used to draw up before a battle. He saw things better in person than on paper. "I'll study it and get back to you."

"Very well." If she was disappointed, she hid it well. "It's time for me to get to class. I'll expect you in about half an hour, then, after I've called roll?"

Overriding his protests, she paid her bill and left, taking all the morning brightness with her. He shivered in her absence and set about making his plans for the rest of the day. After he finished at the school, he would go to Stowe to see if any of their stores sold a hair tonic like the one the robbers used. So far, Dixon hadn't been able to identify it.

As much as he might like to spend the day with Miss Farley, he had work to do.

❧

Clara looked at the second hand creeping around the clock. She had never called a class to order so quickly. Five minutes remained until she had asked Daniel to arrive. Nicholas Whitson's father had declined the invitation. What could they do to fill in the time? They had already read scripture and recited the Lord's Prayer.

An idea jumped to her mind. "While we are waiting for our special guest, I'm going to give you a quote. Raise your hand if you think you know who said it."

What had she done? Did she know them well enough herself? Of course she did. She had excelled in oratory at school and loved stirring patriotic speeches the best of all. Marshalling her thoughts, she pronounced, " 'We hold these truths to be self-evident, that all men are created equal, that they are endowed by their Creator with certain unalienable Rights, that among these are Life, Liberty and the pursuit of Happiness.' "

Little Libby Whitson raised her hand first. "It's from—"

"Wait until I call on you, Libby." Clara hated to douse her enthusiasm, but rules had to be followed for the contest to be fair. "You raised your hand first, Libby. You may answer. But if you are incorrect, I will ask someone else for the answer." She nodded for Libby to speak.

"That's from the Declaration of Independence. By Thomas Jefferson."

That girl deserved a gold star. "That's right, Libby. How about, 'I regret that I have but one life to give for my country'?" Clara was pleased to see that young Phineas Tuttle—Daniel's nephew—raised his hand a fraction of a second before Libby.

"Yes, Phineas?"

"Nathan Hale, ma'am, when them Brits were about to execute him."

"Exactly right. Well done." She beamed. She heard a creak at the back of the room and saw Daniel slip in. He motioned for her to continue.

"How about, 'We the People of the United States,

in Order to form a more perfect Union, establish Justice, insure domestic Tranquility, provide for the common defense, promote the general Welfare, and secure the Blessings of Liberty to ourselves and our Posterity, do ordain and establish this Constitution for the United States of America.'"

"That's easy." Libby frowned. "That's from the—"

"Libby—" Clara warned her.

"The preamble to the Constitution!" Phineas finished.

Would those two young ones compete with each other all the way through school the way she and Daniel had? She wanted her seminary because of girls like Libby with bright, inquiring minds, who deserved a broader education than the public school provided. "You are correct. Remember to raise your hands. Who wrote the preamble?"

Libby's hand shot up first, and Clara nodded for her to speak. "It was written by Gouverneur Morris"

"And the year?" Clara noticed Phineas squirming in his seat.

Libby frowned. "17. . .uh. . .98?" A note of uncertainty crept into her voice. Clara had noticed she sometimes reversed her letters.

Phineas shot to his feet. "It was 1789, Miss Farley."

"You're both right. I have one last quote for you. Every one of you should know this one. Who said, 'In the name of the Great Jehovah and the Continental Congress!'"

No one raised their hands for a moment. Phineas's hand started to go up, but he pulled it down.

"I know the answer to that one." Daniel moved forward from the back door, where he had waited. "Ethan Allen, leader of our own Green Mountain Boys during our War for

Independence, right before he captured Fort Ticonderoga."

The class groaned.

"With Miss Farley's permission, I'd like to give you one last quote."

She nodded.

He stood with his feet shoulder-width apart. " 'Four score and seven years ago our fathers brought forth, upon this continent, a new nation, conceived in liberty, and dedicated to the proposition that "all men are created equal."' "

Clara knew, but no one in the class raised their hands. "Let's think about it, class. A score means the same thing as twenty. If we make it into a math problem"—she took chalk in her hand and went to the blackboard—"we'd have to say—"

Young Tommy Tooms's hand went up. "Four twenties. Eighty."

"Plus?"

"Seven," Daniel prompted.

"Eighty-seven," Tommy said. "And he said eighty-seven years ago, so we'd have to subtract the number, right?"

"Very good, Tommy!" Clara wrote 1864 at the top of the board and the minus sign with 87 below it. "What's the answer?"

Tommy's hand went up again, but Clara nodded to Anna Preston this time. "One thousand seven hundred seventy-seven."

Clara covered her smile. "Or as we call the year, 1777. What was happening back in 1777?"

"He was talking about the War for Independence." Daniel smiled. "He mentioned a new nation, liberty, and equality."

Phineas's hand went up next. "How do we know he said it in 1864?"

"Excellent question, Phineas." Clara was pleased Daniel's nephew thought to ask.

"He actually spoke the words last November, in 1863. Any guesses?" Daniel looked up and down the rows of students.

Daniel's choice of quotation surprised Clara. She'd thought he planned to avoid discussing the battles of the recent war, but she played up to his game. "I believe I know the answer. President Lincoln spoke those words at Gettysburg, where one of the worst battles in the war took place. They dedicated a national cemetery there. He said, 'The brave men, living and dead, who struggled here, have consecrated it.' He wanted to honor the people who gave their lives." She paused, realizing she was speaking in place of Daniel.

Tommy turned his attention to Daniel. "Is that where you lost your arm?"

nine

The eye of every student in the small schoolroom fastened on his stump. Daniel cleared his throat. "No, I lost my arm in a later battle."

Clara poured a glass of water and brought it to him, apology weeping from her eyes. "I'm all right," he whispered.

She clasped her hands together and faced her students. "Class, please give a warm welcome to our guest today, Captain Daniel Tuttle."

"Are you going to tell us about that battle?" Tommy persisted.

"No." That boy must be one of the ones Clara had warned him about. "I only wanted to remind us all that men— and women"—he glanced at Clara, who gave him a small smile—"came to the New World seeking freedom. They were prepared to fight, and die if need be, to defend it."

He studied the assembly. Young Libby had the beak nose of the Whitsons. Others, all freckles and smiles, hailed from the Frisk family. A few of his younger relatives were in attendance, as well. Others he didn't recognize.

"When did your families come to Maple Notch?"

Dates ranged from 1763—when the town was first settled, at the end of the French and Indian War—to as recently as 1862, when the Beatons had taken over the pastorate of the church.

"If you count the French and Indian War, which ended

just before my great-grandparents came here, the men of Maple Notch have been involved in five wars." He lifted up one finger. "My great-grandfathers fought in that first war, and earned the land they built their farms on. They won the land from the French and made Vermont an English colony.

" 'Tweren't but a dozen years later that we were fighting again." He lifted his second finger. "My great-uncle died at the second battle of Fort Ticonderoga, fighting so we could be a free country."

He saw several children, especially among the lads, squirming in the seats, bursting to speak. He recognized a hawk-nosed lad. "I'd guess you're a Whitson." Something triggered in his mind, and he set it aside for later.

"Yes, sir, Nicholas Whitson. My great-granddaddy fought in the Revolutionary War."

Cries of "mine, too!" rang across the room, and he nodded. "And that's why we're here today, and we have a flag with thirty-five stars—including the thirteen states who claimed to have left our country." He lifted his third finger. "Britain didn't want to let us go. So we ended up fighting them again in 1812. My father fought in that war."

He looked at the flag, the same patriotic fervor swelling in his breast that had led him to enlist when they still thought the war would be over by Christmas. If he had to do it all over again, he would. "And now here we are, fighting another battle to prove *all* men are created equal. Even if their skin is a different color. I went off to fight. A lot of men from Vermont did. Yes, I lost my arm, but I consider myself fortunate. Other men, men I considered my friends, lost their *lives*."

He walked behind a diorama a previous class had erected to illustrate the crossing of the Delaware River by George Washington. "All those battles you study about? People like me, your fathers, uncles, and grandfathers fought in them. We fought because we believed freedom was worth dying for. And some of you may well do the same."

As fast as the words had come to him, they left, and he stopped. "And I guess that's all I have to say."

He looked at Clara, who returned his gaze with an amazement that made her eyes even larger than her glasses normally did.

The children stood and clapped while Clara stayed rooted to her spot. When at last they stopped and the silence grew uncomfortable, she joined him in front of the class. "Thank you for reminding us of the price that has been paid so that we may remain free. You have given us a lot to think about. And now, class, we must say good-bye."

She began clapping again, and the children joined in, quieter this time. Her eyes strayed to the back door. He had been so focused on her face, on the lights dancing across the planes of her cheeks below the rims of her glasses, that he hadn't noticed the door opening. Dixon stood there, gesturing for his attention.

Daniel headed for the back, shaking hands as he walked down the aisle. Dixon leaned close to his ear and lowered his voice. "They've hit the bank again."

☙

Clara had followed Daniel to offer him her thanks, so she heard Dixon's announcement. She hoped the clapping kept the news from the children. She bent forward. "My prayers go with you," she whispered.

"Your brother is safe," Dixon assured her before he left.

She took a deep breath and turned around. "And now, class, here is what I want you to do." The wind blew at her back as Daniel departed with Dixon, leaving her cold and alone and a little afraid.

The Lord is with you, she reminded herself. *Don't be afraid.* The children depended on her. Even young Tommy Tooms, who towered at least half a foot taller than she did and hadn't finished growing.

"I have an assignment for you to complete by tomorrow."

Groans erupted around the classroom.

"I think you'll like this one. I want you to talk with your fathers—"

Anna Preston's face fell, and Clara remembered her father had died before she was born.

"Or uncles or grandfathers about your family's history with the army and navy. Your mothers may know the stories, too. Like Captain Tuttle's family, most of your families have sacrificed to make us free. I'll leave a note for Miss Stone, so she will know what we have been doing." If Clara taught tomorrow, she'd write up the stories in a blank book.

Time for morning recess had come, but Clara hesitated to let the children outside with the commotion of more bank robbers on the loose. If only she could go and find out what had happened herself. The hours until the end of school would drag by. Perhaps Mrs. Beaton could spell her at lunch, and she could take a break.

The children glanced to the windows, expecting their recess.

"Before we take recess this morning, I want to start our lessons." She assigned some of the students the math examples on the board; the oldest she gave the task of using their spelling words in a sentence. "Remember you will be judged for penmanship as well as spelling." She brought the youngest ones forward with her.

Later, while the children donned their cloaks, Clara checked outside the building. Discovering all was quiet, she led the children down a short trail to a dell she remembered from childhood. They had behaved so well during the extended session, she allowed them a few extra minutes to run out their energy.

Poor Daniel. He had spoken so bravely about the war, and now, once again, he faced an enemy. She filled the minutes with prayers for him, for his safety, for the apprehension of the men responsible for the robbery.

The children returned to the schoolhouse in good spirits, and she rotated the assignments. Before they started, she said, "I have another special treat in store for you today. If you finish your work in time, I'm going to read one of my very favorite stories at the end of school."

She took the middle group through the McGuffy Readers while the little ones practiced spelling words. She challenged them to think of as many words that had a long *O* as they could. "The one who spells the most correctly will get a special prize." She smiled at them. They nudged each other and set to work. The oldest ones outlined the second chapter of their history book and discussed a group project to teach it to the rest of the school.

At last, lunchtime came, and Mrs. Beaton arrived so that Clara could have a break. She grabbed her lunch sack and headed outside. Ordinary quiet sounds greeted her, as if nothing evil could assault her town. But it had. She cut across the common at her fastest pace, eager to see Lewis. Dixon said he wasn't hurt, but he could be suffering even if he didn't receive a scratch.

Why had the robbers struck a second time? At least the St. Albans' raid made some kind of twisted sense. To Clara's way of thinking, this second robbery confirmed Confederates didn't rob the Bailey Bank, but rather locals intent on mischief.

Finding the bank door locked, Clara knocked at the entrance. Mr. Simeon himself came to the door. "Miss Farley, please come in. We've been expecting you, although I wasn't sure when you'd be able to get away."

"Thank you. I can't stay very long." She slipped past him into the obscurity of the cavernous room. A light gleamed beneath a door at the far side of the building.

"This way." Simeon led her around the obstacles in the way and opened the door. Lewis, a little pale, waved when he saw her. She rushed to his side and hugged him.

"I'm fine, Clara." He managed a weak smile.

She sensed his embarrassment and let him go. "What happened?"

"I. . .had to answer a call of nature." His face reddened deeper than a ripe tomato.

"Don't let him say that. He was our hero." Simeon took his seat behind his desk. "When he saw the horses outside, he came in the back way to warn us. They grabbed him and held the pistol to his temple." The banker sounded as proud as if he were boasting about his own son. "Not that we needed any encouragement. No man's life is worth any amount of money." He lowered his voice, although who he thought would hear him in the enclosed room, she couldn't guess.

"We transferred money from one of our other accounts to help cover the losses. Now. . .now." He shook his head.

"He thinks one of us must have tipped off the robbers, since no one but bank employees knew about the transfer." Lewis shrugged his shoulders. "If you think I did it, just look at my sister's face. She didn't expect this. I didn't even tell her about your plans."

"It's *awful*." Miss Simington, an older woman who had worked at the bank for as long as Clara could remember, twisted her handkerchief in her hands. "We're questioning each other when we need to stand together."

"Now, Eunice, I think you at least should stay home until this—danger—has passed." Simeon patted her hand like an affectionate older brother.

"But I've opened the bank every Thursday morning for the past twenty years, while you have your breakfast meeting with your directors. It's my job." She sniffed back tears. "Will we open for business tomorrow?"

From the glances over the poor woman's head, Clara guessed the question had been asked and answered before. "You have a lot to discuss, and I need to get back to the school." She wished she could have seen Daniel as well, but he must have left to chase the robbers. "I am praying for all of you."

Lewis escorted her through the dark lobby to the front door. In privacy, he hugged her to the bone. "I was scared I would never see you again." He grasped her hands. "Wait for me before you go home. I don't want you wandering the roads alone."

"That does seem the wisest course." Leaving, she waved to him as she walked across the common as she had thousands of times before. She wished Daniel could escort her home. *Shame on you, Clara Farley.* So what if he had expressed extra interest in her over the past few days? The responsibility for the safety of all of Maple Notch weighed on his shoulders.

❧

Daniel and Dixon stopped at the bridge that crossed the river to his family's farm before continuing on the road down to Burlington. "You go on ahead to the other side." He motioned for his companion to continue.

The signs outside the bank had suggested the robbers split up when they left the bank. Daniel and Dixon had followed the clearest trail, headed west. His other deputies went after the other trails.

The robbers started on the main road, but soon their horses' hoofprints became obscured in the heavy traffic that passed along the road. He and Dixon scoured the sides of the road for any signs that the robbers might have headed into the woods. All that effort only resulted in lost time. People had crossed and crisscrossed this part of town so often over the past hundred years that it would take a mind reader to interpret the signs.

The people of Maple Notch might have named an ex-soldier as their constable, but he was no expert in detection. Give Daniel a target, and he could shoot with deadly aim. He used to be real handy in a fistfight, too, but he had yet to figure out how to make up for his missing arm. He couldn't think of a solid reason they had hired him. As soon as he had finished the six months they had offered him, he'd have to figure out what to do with the rest of his life. He wasn't cut out to be a policeman.

Below him, water rippled over rocks, a gentle October

flow. The river could cover a multitude of sins when it came to escape. He nosed around the bushes that hid the bank, checking for any broken stems or torn leaves that might suggest horses had left the road to cross the riverbed.

He heard the *clip-clop* of hooves on the bridge and Dixon emerged. Daniel looked at him, but Dixon shook his head. "No luck."

The wind stirred, and Daniel heard an unexpected sound that made him think of another possibility. "Hold on a minute while I check something." He approached the bank and crouched down to peer under the bridge, but it was too dark to make out anything. He'd have to get underneath and check it out.

"Let me." Dixon came alongside, but Daniel shook his head. A stubborn streak a mile wide wouldn't let him admit he couldn't still do the things he had done before the war. He might not have two hands to grab on to outcroppings anymore, but he was taller now than he was as a boy. He sat down and wiggled forward as far as possible before he jumped. His left arm flailed helplessly at the bank during the short drop. He couldn't seem to stop those involuntary reflexes.

"Are you all right?" Dixon's voice trailed after Daniel, but he didn't answer. He dropped to his belly and crawled forward, keeping out of sight of the dark underbelly of the bridge. With about two yards to go, he stopped moving, listening for movement. This close, the water sounded louder, a small whirlpool circling where it pushed past the pylons. A lone woodpecker knocked against a nearby tree.

Wood creaked overhead. Daniel tensed, watching for movement. None came, and he decided it must have been the wind whistling through cracks in the floor of the bridge. The next time he went to the farm, he'd tell Hiram the bridge needed some repair.

Daniel crept closer, coming up on his knees and grabbing his pistol as he prepared to expose himself to anyone who might be lurking. Silently he counted *three, two, one* and plunged ahead, weapon pointed straight ahead. A raccoon ran past him, chattering about the disruption, dropping his prize on his way past. No other life forms greeted him.

The small round object the raccoon had dropped gleamed like a drop of sunlight on the ground, and Daniel's heart beat faster. Raccoons liked to collect shiny things. Taking a stick, he cleared the space around the object until its outlines became clear: one bright gold coin.

He let out a low whistle. He couldn't prove this coin belonged to the bank batch, of course. But he'd guess he could search every person in town that day and not a one of them would have gold on his person. Once he pocketed the gold piece, he studied the area underneath the bridge for other signs of the robbers' passage. The bridge had become a favorite spot for people for all kinds of reasons. Town frolics found their way there year round.

As a boy, he had hidden under the bridge, waiting for courting couples to pass by. People called it the "kissing bridge," claiming if a man took his time crossing it, he could steal two kisses from his gal. Deep gray eyes hidden behind thin glass frames swam into Daniel's mind, and he imagined her lips soft beneath his.

He chased the thought away. He didn't discover anything else, but he'd bet his bottom dollar that the robbers had passed overhead. He crawled from beneath the bridge and stared up the bank.

Dixon stood there, rope ready in his hands. "Thought you could use this to help you get up." That was Dixon, helping Daniel without making him feel helpless. He grabbed the rope with his good arm, found his footing, and managed to scramble up the bank.

As soon as Daniel crowned the top, a wide grin broke out on his face. "Look what the raccoon found for us," he said as he took the hankie out of his pocket and unwrapped the coin.

Dixon held the coin up to the light and pinged it with his finger. "That's the real thing, all right."

In the bright noon sunshine, Daniel saw fluff caught in the ridges of the coin. "Be careful with that. It's probably just the sack the robber carried it in, but I'll check it out. Maybe we'll get lucky." He pocketed the coin again. "Come on. They went over the bridge."

In the half light of the bridge, Daniel couldn't see any details. "I'll have to come back with a light. I'll borrow a lantern from Hiram when we come back." He rubbed his hand across his forehead. "If we had come straight ahead instead of stopping for every bent twig, we might have caught them here."

"You did what you thought was best," Dixon said. "Don't beat yourself up over it."

Daniel's attention snagged on a much-marked spot on the wall: the courting plank. Nearly every couple in Maple Notch carved their initials there, ever since his parents had started the tradition when his father had built the bridge. His grandparents were there, too, carved when the plank was still a tree growing in the woods. He came from a proud lineage, but what would they think if they could see the mess he had made of the robbery?

Clara would say they wouldn't have done any better. They were ordinary people, not ancient Greek gods. He smiled to himself at the thought. Forget mythology. Neither did they have the wisdom of Solomon nor the strength of Samson.

Maybe lunch at his brother Hiram's house would help him figure out the next step.

&.

" 'He loved his country as no other man has loved her; but no man deserved less at her hands.' " Clara closed the pages of the magazine. Young Libby had tears in her eyes, and no one spoke a word.

The children had held Clara to her promise. When they finished early, she pulled out the December issue of the *Atlantic Monthly* to the opening pages. The anonymous story "The Man without a Country" affected her class the same way it had touched her when she read it for the first time. Philip Nolan, the man condemned to live with his outburst that "I wish I may never hear of the United States again," became both the most pitiable and noblest of patriots before his death.

"One more thing."

Around the classroom, groans erupted.

"I am going to ask Miss Stone to give you extra credit if you bring back an essay about all the reasons why you love the United States." She smiled. "You are dismissed."

The children piled out of the classroom quickly, all except one. Libby crept close to her. "Can I find that story in a book? 'Cause I know I can't borrow your magazine."

Clara shook her head. "As far as I know, it's only been

published in this magazine." She looked at the pages she held in her hand and debated. Did she dare let go of them long enough for Libby to copy the story? She knew from sad experience that lending a book often meant she would never see it again.

She looked into the girl's bright eyes and burned with purpose to see *this* girl expand her knowledge. "I must hold on to this copy for future classes, but I will write out the story and give it to you." She tapped the magazine against her chin. "I may even be able to get a copy from one of my friends."

"You would do that for me?" Libby's feet danced with excitement.

"I would." Clara thought of Daniel's practice of reading from the Bible morning and evening before he would read anything else. "But I want you to promise me something."

"What is it?" Libby looked like she would run to St. Albans and back.

"Promise me you'll read your Bible every day. We both love a good story, but only God's words will last forever."

"I will do that. Thank you, Miss Farley!" Libby made it as far as the door before she turned around again. "I like Miss Stone, but I wish you were our teacher."

Clara hoped she would teach Libby again someday, at her own school. From the door, she watched her students scatter to the four winds. Should she have dismissed them with robbers about? Surely the criminals wouldn't harm innocent children.

The bank hours usually ended half an hour after school let out, but Clara didn't know about today, with the robbery. She would copy the story for Libby while she waited after she walked around the town green. At her school, she would move as many classes into outdoor learning experiences as she could.

She had circled the green once when Lewis headed in her direction from the road leading to their house. She moved to meet him. "Did they let you leave early?"

Lewis nodded. "Mr. Tuttle said there wasn't anything left worth guarding, so I might as well go home. He looked pretty discouraged."

A stone settled in Clara's heart. Did this latest development mean he had lost his depositors' money?

"You didn't have to come back for me. You could have sent a message, and I would have found another way home."

"No." He smiled at her. "I am taking you out to dinner tonight. You've put in a hard day with those young critters and deserve to relax."

"Where did you get the money to pay for a meal?"

"I'm a working man now." He cocked his thumbs on his shoulders.

"You should keep that money."

"Clara." He sounded exasperated. "You take care of me all the time. Let me do something for you for once." In that moment, he looked just like Papa, and her heart melted.

"Very well. This one time." She accepted his arm and walked with him to the café.

ten

Late-afternoon sunshine poured through the windows, giving the interior of the café a warm, friendly feeling. At midafternoon, Clara and Lewis were the only customers.

The bell on the door rang as they entered the room. "Just a minute," Fannie called from the kitchen.

Lewis took advantage of the delay to walk down the counter. "Look at that pie. Mmhmm." He grinned at Clara.

"I don't want dessert."

"Of course you do. This is my treat, remember?" He grinned again. "Pumpkin pie or spice cake. A hard choice."

"Eat your meal first." She used her best schoolmarm voice. "You shouldn't eat dessert unless you clean your plate."

He arched an eyebrow. "Yes, ma'am!"

Fannie came from the kitchen. "Miss Farley!" She blinked twice. "I don't often have the pleasure of your company twice on the same day."

Would the overly talkative waitress tell the world Clara Farley was a spendthrift, not to mention too lazy to cook a meal?

"And Mr. Farley." Fannie relaxed her face into her best simper. "I heard about your bravery at the bank today. Were you hurt?"

"I didn't do anything special." He bowed in her direction. "Thank you for your concern."

Fannie led them to the front table and rattled off their

choices. "If you care to wait until after four, you may choose from our dinner menu."

"What say you?" Lewis asked.

"That's only half an hour from now. It will be getting dark before we head home. . . ." Clara chewed her lip. "But why not? My brother doesn't take me out to dinner all that often." For tonight, she would relax and pretend Fannie believed she had a dozen lads chasing her. Even if one was her brother.

"Then we will each have a bowl of soup for now, and we'll be your first dinner customers." Lewis turned on a smile full of sunshine and charm, one Clara recognized from long experience.

In spite of Lewis's good humor, Clara wished a man of more serious demeanor could join her for dinner this evening. Daniel had no one to fix him a hot meal, to take care of him after his hard day. She suppressed the desire to jump up from the table and take a hot plate over to the Bailey house.

The town constable occupied altogether too much of her thoughts recently.

પ્ર

Lunch with Hiram provided no answers to Daniel's questions, but at least he left with a full stomach and a pan full of leftovers.

"You're too thin. You need to marry some nice young woman and let her take care of you." Hettie piled enough food for a week on his plate.

"Hush, woman." Hiram chuckled. "Don't take any mind of Hettie's fussing. She just wants the best for you."

Later, after they finished eating, Hiram followed Daniel out to the barn, where he fed the horse a handful of oats. "I know you think no one will have you. But I bet Hettie could find half a dozen women between now and Sunday dinner who would be more than willing to take a chance on you."

Daniel felt like jumping on the horse's back and dashing down the road as fast as the gelding could gallop. But he wouldn't treat his brother that way. "Don't even suggest that."

"There's someone." Amusement laced Hiram's voice. "Someone has finally caught your eye."

"It's nothing." Daniel fiddled with the saddle straps.

"There *is* someone." Hiram tapped his chin. "But who? You've talked with nearly every female in Maple Notch since the robberies began." His eyes, as dark a brown as their father's had been, searched Daniel's for clues. "But it's none of them." He snapped his fingers. "I know. You have been doing business with Miss Farley."

A muscle in Daniel's cheek quivered at the mention of her name, and heat scampered up his neck and into his cheeks.

"Miss Clara Farley." Hiram shook his head. "She's a bit thin and spinsterish for my taste, but—"

"She's no spinster." When Daniel saw the mirth in his brother's eyes, he knew he had revealed more than he intended. "I saw her at the school today. Miss Stone is sick." He looked sideways at his brother. "Now, that one *is* a spinster."

Hiram snickered.

"Phineas performed well. You should be proud." By the time Daniel finished detailing his nephew's accomplishments, he had derailed Hiram's interest in Clara. Or so he hoped.

"Hettie will see Clara at the ladies' meeting next week." Hiram clapped Daniel on the back as they headed out of the barn. "I'll ask her to do some sleuthing of her own."

Of all the. . . Daniel wished the subject had never come up with Hiram. But with his father gone, his oldest brother tried to take his place. Daniel shouldn't resent his. . .concern. But no one in the Tuttle family had ever needed a marriage broker, and they wouldn't start with him. Not if he could help it.

Then you need to speak to Clara of your interest before someone else spills the beans.

That thought scared Daniel more than all the enemies he had faced in battle.

❧

Daniel put his brother's interference out of his mind to consider how best to pursue the robbers. Had they headed south, down toward Lake Champlain and New York? Headed up river and crossed back at the next bridge?

The circle of suspects had tightened, limited to the people aware of the gold shipment. That included a handful of people on the Burlington end and a slightly larger number at this end, as well as anyone they might have told. He'd have to ask Simeon for a complete list. A conversation with his brother was his best choice, since trailing the robbers had proved useless. By now, they could have circled back and arrived home as if they had never left. His shoulders slumped. He was useless as a lawman.

Once he arrived in town, he headed straight for Simeon's house, a few blocks away from the bank. His brother opened the door before he knocked. "I've been expecting you." Simeon looked resigned when Daniel reported his lack of progress. He provided Daniel with a list of all his employees, which exceeded two dozen people in all. Another two hours passed while they sifted through who knew about the shipment, who had been at work, and who had the day off, but at last Daniel had as much information as Simeon could provide.

"If you had to guess?" Daniel prodded.

"Believe me, I've thought of very little else." Simeon shrugged. "I don't want to think any of them are guilty, but someone must be. Let me sleep on it overnight. There's something niggling at my mind, but I can't quite place it."

The following morning, Daniel stopped by the café for his usual breakfast. "Will Miss Farley be joining you this morning?" Fannie asked as she ushered him to a small table toward the back corner. He smiled to himself. Alone, he didn't get the same special treatment he had received yesterday. Bright curiosity rimmed her eyes. Had the community started linking his name with Clara's on the basis of a single meal?

"No."

"She's been coming in real regular. She was here last night with that handsome brother of hers." Fannie's smile said she had succumbed to Lewis's charms. With his charm, he might marry before his sister did. Some men had all the luck.

Or all the trouble. He smiled at the memory of his father's cheerful warning against marrying in haste and repenting at leisure. Marriage to a woman like Clara wouldn't be easy, but he would never get bored, either.

Daniel's stomach clutched. He wanted to see Clara again, but not here, where all the ears of Maple Notch could hear their private business. Perhaps he should go to her home, since he needed to speak with Lewis about his whereabouts over the past two days.

When Fannie poured his coffee, she took something out of her pocket and rubbed it with her apron. "Will you take a look at this?" She handed him a gold coin, as shiny as the day it had left the mint.

She dropped the coin in Daniel's palm, where it burned like it had just left the refiner's fire.

ફ્રેં

When Clara awoke in the morning, the sun had already risen. Surprised Lewis hadn't invited her to join him for breakfast, she threw on a dressing gown and checked his room. He lay motionless in his bed.

"Lewis! Get up!"

He opened one eye. "Oh, it's you." He closed it again.

"Your job!" She sat next to him on the bed and nudged him in the side.

"The bank won't be open today. Mr. Tuttle told me he'd send word when he needs me again."

She threw her hands in the air. "I wish you had told me last night." If the bank closed for several days, when would she have a chance to speak with Mr. Simeon about leasing the house? With days sliding toward November and winter weather, she might not be able to open the school in the spring as she had hoped.

"Sorry."

Clara sniffed. A faint odor of liquor wafted through the air, and she got down on her knees. A partially empty whiskey bottle sat under his bed, right next to a coin purse, much fuller than it should be from two days' work at the bank. She felt its weight in her hand, drawing it out from beneath the bed.

"Wait, Clara, I can explain."

"Later." Grabbing the bottle, she marched out the door, down the stairs, and threw it as far as she could. It smashed with a satisfying thud against a nearby maple tree. She slid down on the front steps and wrapped her arms around her waist. Tears she had held back when her father had died, when her hopes for the school had been delayed and delayed again, when every possible suitor had turned and run, all surfaced at this final indignity.

Lewis came behind her. "Clara, it's not what you think."

"It's exactly what I think. I've blinded myself to your wrongdoings all along. Go. Get out of here. And don't come home until you're ready to make things right."

Lewis put a hand on her shoulder, but she shook it off. He plodded toward the barn, each step hitting her heart hard. The barn door banged, and horse hooves clattered down the lane. Lewis had taken her at her word, and she couldn't call him back.

Clara knew all this without watching, even though she curled herself into a ball, trying not to see or hear or feel. No feelings at all would be better than the despair that overwhelmed her.

"Clara!" A different voice, a beloved voice promised comfort and succor. *Daniel.* "What happened to you?"

A small part of her came alive at the sound of his voice, the part that wanted to enjoy sunshine and sing for joy. She opened her eyes and unwound her arms from around her middle. She looked into eyes fiery with compassion and worry—for her. He took her fingers in his right hand. Shivering, she glanced at the place where their arms touched. . .and saw the ribbons dangling from the end of her dressing gown. Her hand shot to her mouth. "I'm not dressed."

He chuckled. "I noticed. Do you feel well enough to get into some clothes?"

"I have to." She dashed inside and up the stairs, passing a full length mirror as she did so. Rather than horror, the figure that she saw bespoke of feminine allure. Oh, not her curves. Her nightdress, while not appropriate attire, was modest enough. But color flushed her cheeks and her hair framed her naked face, her gray eyes sparkling with the wash of her recent tears. She looked almost. . .pretty. In light of the heartrending start to her morning, the sight mocked her.

She poured water into a basin and scrubbed her face until it gleamed from the effort, tear stains banished. A quick brush of her hair sufficed before putting it in a bun. Last of all she slipped into her blackest outfit, as befitting her mood.

When she went downstairs, she hoped Daniel hadn't left. She found him in the kitchen.

"I made you some coffee." He grinned as if it was an old joke. "Café au lait style, or at least my attempt at it."

She smiled, her fakest smile yet, and settled into a chair. "Thank you."

"Have you eaten breakfast?"

"That's none of your concern."

He took one step toward her, smoke gathering in his eyes, and ran his knuckle along her cheekbone. "I'd like to make it my concern, Miss Clara Farley. Anything that troubles you troubles me." Then he smiled again, as if he hadn't just turned her world on its head, and grabbed a handful of eggs from the egg basket. "I'll fry us up some eggs."

Clara put one hand to her cheek, once again hot to touch, her heart seared with the briefest flicker of kindness. She wanted to run and shout to the skies. She wanted to slide through a crack in the floor. What she had to do was decide whether to tell the lawman her suspicions about her brother.

No, she decided. Not unless he asked. She wouldn't lie, but neither would she offer suspicions without proof.

She took a loaf from the breadbox and turned to the knife drawer. Daniel placed his hand over hers. "Breakfast is my treat this morning. You go sit down." Slicing the bread, he held it over a flame as if he had done it forever.

Clara wished he would let her do something so she could calm the riot in her mind. Did he think he could announce "anything that troubles you troubles me" and expect her to be unmoved? To cover her confusion, she sipped the coffee, a perfect dark roast lightened with milk, which warmed her to her toes.

He must have noticed when she finished the cup, because he appeared at her elbow with the coffeepot. "Do you want some more?"

"Yes. It's delicious."

He poured a bit of coffee in the cup and then added milk warmed in a pan before stirring them together. "I understand heating the milk is the secret to a good cup. I'll let you add whatever sugar you want."

After he set breakfast on the table, he carried on light banter while they ate. With each bite, she regained a portion of her equanimity. When she had finished, she felt less frightened of speaking with him, even if not quite ready.

Daniel cleared the table and fixed them both another cup of coffee. "Shall we move to the parlor?" His gentle smile encouraged her to move.

Daniel took the overstuffed chair that was Lewis's favorite seat, and Clara's worries returned. She set down her coffee cup.

He leaned forward. "I am willing to listen to whatever upset you so this morning."

No. I can't. I won't.

He paused, and when she didn't answer, he spoke again.

"But I suspect you're a lot like me. You don't want to talk about it." He raised an eyebrow, and she nodded.

"That's what I thought. So, I'll tell you why I came here instead. I need to talk to Lewis, is all. We're concentrating on—"

"Bank employees. Of course." She couldn't put off the decision any longer. Should she say something or not? "I'm afraid he's not here."

"I noticed his horse was gone when I put my horse in the barn." Daniel sipped his coffee. "When do you expect him home?"

"He doesn't tell me his plans." *I made him leave.* "He may not come back for a few days, since the bank is closed."

"And do you know where he went?"

She shook her head, and he sighed. "Please tell me as much as you know about his movements this week."

"I suggested he apply for the job. Which he did." The fact that it had brought her so much joy at the time now hung heavy in her heart. "He spent the last two days at the bank, and last night he took me out to dinner."

"Dinner at the café. Fannie mentioned that to me this morning." Daniel looked to the window and then back at her. "She said he paid her with this." He reached into his pocket and pulled out a gold coin.

❧

The color that had brightened and softened Clara's face fled in an instant, and Daniel's heart sank. *No, please, no.* He didn't want his suspicions confirmed any more than Clara would want to believe it.

"He said Simeon paid him yesterday." She glanced away.

Daniel turned the coin over in his palm. "Do you know if

he has more coins like this?"

She hesitated. "Not for certain."

He waited her out. He didn't want to put words into her mouth, but silence often provoked further conversation.

"I found a coin purse in his room, but I didn't look in it. For all I know, it's filled with pennies."

"Let's go see, then, shall we?" Without giving her time to protest, he set down his cup and headed for the stairs. He heard her soft tread behind him and paused. "It's that way." He didn't need her to point the way since a faint but perceptible odor of liquor was evident.

Clara followed him as far as the doorway. "The coin purse was underneath the bed." Misery dripped from her voice.

Daniel's hand scooted around the cavity but encountered nothing but a few dust balls. "It's not there. Does he have any other hiding places?"

She hesitated, perhaps unwilling to intrude on her adult brother's privacy. Her mouth thinning in a straight line, she went to the bureau and opened the second drawer, where she pulled out a cigar box from the far corner.

"As a boy, he put his most prized treasures in here." Clara ran her hands over the top. "A never-fail fishing lure. The ribbons he won at school. Any rock that he found especially interesting. That kind of thing." She lifted it to her ear and shook it, as if guessing the contents. "It's too light for anything heavy."

"Let's open it and see, shall we?"

Clara gave it to Daniel, her teeth biting into her bottom lip, and retreated to the door.

The box that had seemed enormous to him as a boy now fit in one hand. He hefted it and looked at the clasp. "Doesn't look like it's been opened for a while." He smiled at her, and the worry on her face lessened by a fraction.

He lifted the cover and breathed a sigh of relief. Nothing there but the mementos of a man's boyhood, darkened by grime deposited over the years. To make certain, he lifted out the items one at a time, checking for anything hidden at the bottom of the box. A sheet of paper, folded in half, detailed a map with X marking the spot of some buried treasure. The crude writing and crayon pronounced the work of a child, not a grown man. Not that he expected Lewis to leave a map to his treasure, in any case.

The thought wouldn't leave him alone, though. What had worked well before might serve the same purpose a second time. He and Clara needed to go on a treasure hunt.

eleven

"Do you know anything about this?" Daniel handed Clara the map. He headed out the bedroom door and back down the stairs. He heard a slight giggle and relaxed.

"Lewis was fascinated by the stories of the famous pirate LaFitte." Her face softened, and he saw traces of the young girl she had been. "Papa told him no pirates ever came to Vermont, that we don't even have an ocean here, but Lewis loved to pretend. He spent an entire summer searching for buried treasure. Whenever I needed to find him, I'd have to follow his latest treasure map."

"Did he bury treasure of his own?" Daniel wiggled his eyebrows.

"Of course!" She covered her mouth with her hand. "Oh."

Daniel took a deep breath. He wished he didn't have to ask the next question. "Can you find the spot marked on this map?"

"But he was just a child. . . ." Her voice trailed away. "I know exactly where it is. Come with me."

She could have avoided the question, but Clara wasn't that kind of woman. Tension screamed from her shoulders, as rigid as a plumb line, but she led him outside. "The big red box is the barn, of course." She pointed to an overgrown field to the west. "And the round green circle is the field Papa let lie fallow. Behind that are the trees. The black circle is the well, or rather, where the well used to be." She studied the map again, a crude X covering a field of purple and blue.

"He dug his hole in a patch of wildflowers. He made me mad when he destroyed all that beauty for pretend treasure. It's this way." Without warning, she took off across the yard, and he let her take the lead. Right now, she'd welcome his company about as much as a polecat.

She led him about a five-minute walk into the woods, far enough to feel like an adventure to a small boy. The place where she stopped looked a lot like the woods around them.

"I believe this is the place, although it's hard to tell." She gazed into the tree branches. "The tree has grown since then, but I see the crook where I used to climb." Her face colored. "I spent a summer climbing trees before I decided no girl should do such a thing." She shook her head. "Whatever he buried is in this spot. There's only one problem." She gestured. "Neither one of us brought a digging tool."

"That's all right." Daniel bent down to examine the spot. "No one has dug here for years. We'd know if there had been any recent activity."

The last of the worry lines disappeared from Clara's face. "Then he hasn't been here." She acted like it proved Lewis's innocence, but then her shoulders slumped. "Not that that means anything."

Daniel put his good arm around her shoulders. "Let's head back. Things will sort themselves out." She allowed his embrace, leaning into him, and his heart sang.

❧

Clara welcomed Daniel's strength of mind, of character, of body. How tired she was of doing things on her own, taking care of a brother like a parent instead of being his older sister and friend. She made no move to put space between her and Daniel, lost in their own private Camelot. She could rest there forever. All too soon they reached the fields and then the yard. He let go of her shoulder and opened the door to the barn.

She lit a lamp to chase the shadows. If only she could find a lantern of truth to light the way through the mess with Lewis. She looked out the open door, willing him to return with an innocent explanation. In her heart, she knew that wouldn't happen.

"Even if he is involved, he didn't act alone." Daniel shuffled his feet.

She turned a snort into a hiccup. "Does that make it any better?"

"Maybe not in the eyes of the law, but it matters to me. Sometimes a group of men will do things they would never do as individuals." His eyes grew dark, and she wondered if some dark memory haunted him.

He shook himself and walked to the back wall. "Are these yours?" He pointed to a pair of heavy saddlebags.

She shook her head. "They belong to Lewis."

"Do you mind?" Assuming her assent, he lifted the bags from the peg and brought them to her. As soon as he opened the bag, odors assaulted her. The condensed aroma of tobacco and whiskey cleared her breathing, and spices reminiscent of church and kitchen tickled her memory— Lewis's cologne.

"I'll have to take this with me." Daniel didn't move, his forage cap in his hand. "I won't tax your conscience and make you promise to tell me when you see Lewis again. I will leave that between the two of you and God." He looked at her then, and the sad smile on his face made her tingle all over.

She wanted to throw herself into his arms, to promise him

the moon, but she couldn't. "I appreciate that."

He handed her the map, letting his hand linger a moment longer than necessary before he grabbed the reins of his horse. The horse moseyed toward the barn door, keeping pace with her steps. After mounting the horse, Daniel paused. "I meant what I said earlier. Every word." He bent over and kissed the top of her head. Then with a kick into the sides of the horse, he burst into the sunshine and headed away from Clara.

She wandered into the house, dazzled and dazed. She looked in the same mirror that had reflected her in her dressing gown earlier. The same rosy cheeks and bright eyes stared back at her. She patted the top of her head, where she could feel the imprint of his kiss. Before she could change her mind at such a foolish act, she grabbed a pair of scissors and cut a small swatch of hair from the crown of her head and slipped it into a locket. Not until she finished cleaning up the breakfast dishes did she realize they hadn't once discussed her plans for the school. Where had her brain disappeared when it mattered? Hiding in the shadow of her heart, apparently. If she couldn't get Daniel Tuttle out of both heart and head, she might have to find another place to start her school.

From then on, the day worsened. The promising sunshine of early morning clouded over by midafternoon and settled into a perpetual twilight indicative of snow. Where had Lewis gone? She regretted her threat. The last place he needed to go was among people who would encourage further wrongdoing. "Lord, You know where he is. And he is Yours." At least she thought Lewis was a Christian. As a boy, he had gone forward at a revival meeting and been baptized. For a time, he hungered for spiritual things as much as she did. What had happened to him?

The hours stretched out like the expanse of the ocean the one time she had seen it. Even *Walden* couldn't hold her attention today. Turning mattresses and adding quilts burned some of her energy before she extracted the *Atlantic Monthly* to copy the story for Libby.

By day's end, snow fell like a fine mist, covering the ground with a crazy quilt design. She went to the barn for the evening chores. The unique aroma of Lewis's cologne seemed to hang in the air, taunting her. How hadn't she recognized it before? Maybe she could blame it on her sniffles.

The door swung open, light outlining a shadowy figure on horseback. Afraid as never before, Clara backed into the far corner, where she hoped the darkness would hide her. But then she recognized the profile and knew her brother had returned.

Lewis whistled, a march that rang in her ears, and she slid down the wall. He had no right to be so happy, not when he had brought such misery on the town.

The time had come for Lewis to take accountability for his actions. She would go to Daniel in the morning and tell him she would help him in any way she could.

❧

"Are you certain about this?"

Clara's determination almost faltered under the kindness of Daniel's gaze, but she held on. "Yes. If he's innocent, I want it proven. And if he's guilty, then. . .I do him no favors by protecting him from the consequences of his actions."

The weight on Clara's heart had lightened when she found Daniel at the jail, since she didn't leave home until after Lewis had left. What if he asked questions about her destination? *Oh, I'm just going into town to talk with Captain*

Tuttle about catching you and the other bank robbers.

"Very well." Daniel drummed his fingers on the desk. "Your timing is perfect. Simeon is joining me in a few minutes to discuss our plans." He stood and retrieved a coffeepot from the stove. "Want a cup? I'll warn you: It's my usual mud. Maybe I should serve it to you in a bowl with a spoon."

She giggled. Trust Daniel to find a way to bring humor to the sad situation. "I'll pass, thank you."

He poured himself a cup and put the pot back on the stove. "I'm surprised you came into town, with the snow last night."

"That dusting wouldn't keep a bear in his den unless he had already settled in for his winter's nap." She didn't know if she was pleased or offended that Daniel saw her as a fragile flower ready to wither at the first sign of bad weather.

He saluted her with the cup.

Silence stretched. "Did you ask about the saddlebags?" She had to know the answer.

Daniel's smile faded. "Beaton recognized the scent. It was the same one he smelled on the day of the robbery."

A sliver of hope disappeared with the answer. Clara glanced at the clock. As the minute hand inched toward the top of the hour, the front door opened, and Simeon Tuttle poked his head in.

"Daniel, I didn't know you had an appointment. I'll come back."

"No, come on in. Miss Farley is going to take part in our discussions."

The banker hid well any surprise he felt. That inexpressive face probably served him well in business. Not Daniel. His eyes ranged between surprise and delight and anger with very little attempt to hide his emotions.

Simeon dragged the only other chair in the room to the front of Daniel's desk and cocked his head in Clara's direction. "How can we help you? We're not ready to finalize the arrangements about the house with the recent problems at the bank."

She shook her head. "That's not why I'm here." A glance at Daniel told her he left the explanation up to her. Tugging her bottom lip between her teeth, she said, "I want to get to the truth about Lewis. If he is involved, and even—Lord be thanked—if he is not. And to identify who else might be responsible."

"Ah." Simeon settled back in his chair and rubbed his chin with his hand. "I appreciate that."

"Daniel—Captain Tuttle—said you had a plan?"

"We worked it out yesterday." Simeon glanced at Daniel, who nodded. "We need to replenish cash in the bank, since they wiped us out."

"Of course."

"Don't look so worried." Daniel smiled at her. "We have a plan."

So you say. "And that is?"

"A decoy." Daniel gestured for his brother to explain.

"I will let it slip that we are expecting a lockbox by carriage tomorrow—on Saturday, when the bank is ordinarily closed. The carriage will stop at the bridge, where the money will be transferred to a single rider."

"Me." Daniel grinned. "As well as a posse of men prepared to take action, but they will be well hidden."

Clara's heart shuddered. The proposal exposed everyone involved to danger.

"We're going to be sure they know exactly where the exchange will take place. When I examined the old bridge yesterday, I noticed a lot of good hiding places. An excellent place for an ambush."

"If robbery is attempted, we'll catch them red-handed." Excitement stripped years from Simeon's countenance.

Clara caught sight of the handcuffs dangling from the wall behind Daniel's desk, ready for the bank robbers. A vision of Lewis dragged off to jail like a common criminal swam before her eyes, but she hardened her heart. He would only be arrested if he was involved. "How can I help?"

Simeon held his hands in front of him, and she noticed how white and clean they were, indicative of someone who worked with his brain and not with his hands. Unlike Daniel's strong, brown hand, which promised single-handed rescue if the need arose. "Please tell Lewis that we need the bank employees back in the morning. I'll send a messenger as well, but I want to reinforce the request."

Daniel blew air from his cheeks and slapped his hand against the heavy desk. "And if you should happen to mention the gold shipment. . ." His eyes grabbed hers, daring her to say no.

The windowless building crowded in on Clara, stealing her breath with its stale odor of past sins and justice applied. "I'll do it." With those words, she stood. "Now, if you'll excuse me." If she didn't leave soon, she'd faint on the spot.

Once outside, deep breaths of the cold autumn air shocked her into alertness. She considered going to Dixon's to check for new books. Before she had decided her next move, Daniel and Simeon left the jailhouse.

As Simeon headed for the bank, Daniel approached her.

"I've thought about your requested changes to the house."

Thoughts swirled in Clara's head for a moment before the change of subject registered. "Good. I've wondered what the status was." She forced a chuckle. "When I wasn't worrying about Lewis."

"Shall we discuss the changes over one of Fannie's fine breakfasts?" He gestured in the direction of the café, a smile warming his face, as if the fact she had agreed to betray her brother didn't matter.

"I already had breakfast, but a cup of coffee would be nice." She laughed. "Real coffee. No offense meant."

"And none taken." He offered her his arm, as if they did this kind of thing every day, and she accepted it.

If they walked arm in arm in plain sight around the common many more times, the town would buzz with gossip of their courtship. Clara allowed herself to look up at his face, his strong chin, matching her strides to his purposeful movements, and she forgot anyone who might be watching.

Good cheer fell like mist when they entered the café; the red and white checkered curtains and the white linen tablecloths made even a lowly breakfast meal feel special. Fannie greeted them at the front. "I'm glad to see you again. We have two cinnamon rolls left. I'll ask Cook to set them aside for you."

Daniel's murmur of approval overrode Clara's protest. Fannie poured coffee without asking while she took his order, the Lumberjack's Special, and then disappeared into the kitchen. He noticed Clara's astonished look. "I may not get any lunch. This'll have to do me."

"You don't need to apologize. Lewis rarely eats breakfast."

At the mention of her brother's name, Daniel's cheeks

darkened, and Clara regretted her comment. She didn't want anything to mar their pleasant exchange. "I'm sorry. I shouldn't have mentioned him."

"Of course you should. He's your brother." Daniel poured cream and sugar into his coffee but paused before stirring it. "Don't make the mistake of thinking all men are like him."

His gaze seared her from the top of her head down to her toes, and she drank from her glass of water to cool off. "I don't." Her voice sounded small, even to herself. She forced her lips into a smile and looked up. "You said you've considered the changes I requested?"

He took a handful of papers from his pocket and unfolded them, evening out the creases as he placed them on the table. "I agree with most of them, but I have alternate suggestions for a couple of your ideas...."

≈

Daniel could have stayed at the café all day. As it was, he put his hand over the top of his coffee cup when Fannie tried to refill it for the fourth time. A few people had already started to wander in for their luncheon.

Discussing the school—both the physical space and Clara's rather radical ideas—brought her to life. Daniel loved watching this Clara. She argued her ideas as skillfully as Lincoln and Douglas in their famous debates, and her voice rose in pitch as she hurled words at Daniel. With every cup of coffee, her speech sped up, and her cheeks blazed with more color until the red and white patches on her face could have provided the inspiration for the checkered pattern of the curtains. Her hands flew in a dozen directions as she explored and explained what she needed for the school. Through her eyes, he could see her vision.

With his refusal of that final cup of coffee, the time had come to go. "So if we are agreed, I'll order supplies from Dixon and arrange for the work to start." A part of him wanted to deny her the school, to instead offer a future with gray-eyed children who would bring his grandparents' house to life again. But no. The man who won Clara's heart must understand the passion that drove her. Daniel would no more snatch that away from her than. . .he would have given his arm if he had had a choice.

But someday, maybe. . .

A man could dream.

Maybe the time for dreaming was over. Maybe it was time for this man to act.

twelve

Daniel rode down the road that connected the Tuttle farm with Maple Notch. Land west of the river that separated them from town had once been mostly wilderness. His great-grandfathers had worked their entire lives to carve holdings out of the forest.

In time, the Tuttle and Reid families multiplied. Now a patchwork of small farms belonging mostly to members of Daniel's family spread west from the river toward Burlington. Hiram lived on his father's land. The family would make room for him if he chose to lay down his badge once his term of office was over.

Daniel knew he could succeed in farming, even if his arm would make adjustments necessary. After all, he had grown up with the rhythms of the seasons, of planting and waiting and harvesting. But his heart didn't lie with the land, nor with the bank, the way Simeon's did. He had come to enjoy his job as constable, even the testing that the robberies brought.

Before he lost his arm, he had considered joining the cavalry to protect the expanding western frontier. But continued military service was no longer an option. Not to mention the reasons he had discovered to stay—especially one gray-eyed beauty.

He paused by the original Reid homestead. Its current resident, one of his cousins, worked in the field, harvesting the last of the pumpkins and winter squash. Would Clara like to be a farmer's wife? Like him, she had grown up on a farm. But her eyes were on a bigger prize—training young women for the future. They both longed for new horizons.

He clucked to his horse and urged him forward. If he didn't live in the Bailey house, and if he didn't want to farm, where would he choose to live? Except for an occasional stand of trees, the wilderness on this side of the river had been transformed to cultivated land. He couldn't hide in a hermit's cabin and live off the land, not here, not like Thoreau talked about in *Walden*.

He reached the bridge. At some point, his father had stopped charging tolls. Simeon reinstituted the practice, stating they needed money to maintain the bridge. Some day the town might take over management of the bridge, but for now, the Tuttle Bridge remained the possession of the family that built it.

His horse pounded onto the bridge, the sound of hooves echoing in the empty space. Not too long from now, Hiram would need to keep the floor snow-packed, so that sleighs could run across the boards unharmed. The wood had dulled to a weathered gray, a sturdy testament to its workmanship.

In the silence, Daniel could sense fiddle music and the shrieks of children. The cold air cleared the scents of horse and food and dirt ground into the boards. If the wood could talk, it would tell the tale of Maple Notch's history. Tomorrow would add another chapter to the ongoing story.

Horse hooves struck the boards and stopped. Sunshine outlined a feminine figure on horseback at the other end of the bridge.

❧

Clara didn't have a good excuse for coming to the bridge.

She only knew that when she didn't find Daniel at the jail, she felt compelled to keep riding west in the direction of the Tuttle farm.

The cold of approaching winter hardened the mud underfoot and made a smooth ride. With no one to report to and no duties for the morning, she indulged in a brisk ride. Miss Featherton would approve of the exercise.

Clara gave Misty her head and let her race, spirit free, just shy of dangerous abandon. Wind whipped her hair and beat her skin, ridding her of any doubts and imperfections. When they reached the rise before the bridge, she pulled Misty up and started again at a slower pace.

"What a glorious day!" As she shook her head, her hair tumbled to her shoulders, and she laughed. When she spotted the Frisk farm, she realized her clothing had gone awry. She tugged her skirts farther down her legs and swept her hair into the hairnet. A few stray hairpins allowed her to pin wisps of curl into place. Horse and rider proceeded at an orderly pace to the bridge. Clara peeked over the edge of the bank, where the river gurgled over a few rocks in its path.

She paused at the entrance to the bridge to allow her eyes to adjust to the light. In here the river sounded louder, almost ready to explode from its banks and run across the fields. She dismounted and took a few steps forward.

"Hello, Clara." A voice spoke out of the semi-darkness.

She jumped back. "Daniel? Is that you?"

"Nobody else here except us mice." Daniel stepped out of the gloom a few yards away from her.

"Mice?" The word came out as a squeak.

"Are you afraid of a few little mice?" He tilted his head, waiting for her answer.

"Let's just say I don't care to run across one unexpected." She moved forward, eyes scanning the walls for any sign of vermin. A mouse skittered by her feet, and she shivered. Approaching, Daniel hung his coat around her shoulders. The warm wool, saturated with his masculine scent, chased away her nervousness.

"Where were you headed? I don't often see you out this way."

Clara didn't want to admit the truth—that part of her hoped to run into him. "I used to ride all over town when I was a girl. Misty could take me home even if I didn't touch the reins, couldn't you, girl?" She leaned over and ran her hand down the mare's neck, and Misty nickered in response. "You've discovered another one of my unwomanly vices. When I was younger, I pulled on Lewis's britches to make riding easier. I've grown up, some." She sighed. "But I still love a good ride. We won't have many more beautiful days like today this year, so I indulged myself."

Daniel chuckled. "I doubt you could hide your gender if you chopped your hair as short as a man's and swore like a sailor." His hand swept up and down. "From the pretty curls on top of your head to your tiny feet, you're all woman."

This time heat started from the roots of her hair and traveled to her shoulders and below. She could only hope the dim light hid her high color. Averting her face from him, her gaze wandered the walls of the bridge. A spit of light shone through the cracks, highlighting spider webs overhead.

Daniel took his place beside her and stared in the same patch of wall. A half smile formed on his face. "I was looking at that just the other day." He tugged her hand in the direction of a scarred plank of wood. Its significance didn't register for a handful of seconds.

"That's—"

"The reason it's called the Courting Bridge. New initials have been added since I left for the war." He peered at some of the newer etchings in the wood. "ID and DR—Isaiah Dixon and Deborah Robson, 1862, unless I miss my guess."

Clara had seen the spot before, of course. Whenever the school picnicked near the bridge, the girls would giggle about who might carve *their* initials on the bridge someday. For someone who knew the parties involved, the couples' plank was better than the church registry as a record of love and marriage in Maple Notch.

Daniel leaned in before shifting a few inches to the side. He ran his fingers along the older marking on the wood, then stopped, his fingernail tipped into a groove. "There it is." He beckoned her closer.

The letters had worn over time. "I'm sorry, is that a *T*?"

"JT and SR. My grandparents, Josiah Tuttle and Sally Reid." His hand dropped by a couple of inches. "And here are my parents—CT and BB."

"Calvin Tuttle and Beatrice Bailey."

He smiled an acknowledgment. "My father discovered the tree when they felled lumber to build the bridge. He added his initials later." He stood back. "Hiram and Simeon are here, too, somewhere." His voice sounded wistful, as if uncertain if he would ever get to add "DT" to the family tree.

And whose initials did he dream of coupling with his on the plank? She could see them, bold, decisive strokes—DT and CF. Tears stung her eyes. In spite of his seeming admiration for her, how could the town constable have any interest in the sister of a common thief?

❧

Daniel felt Clara pulling away from him, when he wanted to hold her close and safe from harm. He had bared his heart; she must know of his interest in her. Unless she was rejecting him. He went cold at the thought.

Somehow in this moment on the bridge, where they seemed as alone in the world as Adam and Eve in the garden, he had hoped for a kiss. For some sign that at least she returned his affection. But when he glanced at her face, her eyes glittered with some dark emotion that left no room for romantic fiddle faddle. She turned in the direction of her horse.

After she climbed onto her horse's back, she faced him. "I'm glad I ran into you. I wanted tell you that Lewis knows the shipment will be coming early tomorrow morning."

Lewis. Daniel wished his name had some *B*s and *T*s, sounds he could spit out of his mouth. The name Lewis sounded weak, like the man. How could he ever hope for a future with Clara as long as her brother stood between them?

"I want to be here when you spring the trap."

An objection rose in Daniel's throat, but he swallowed it down. She didn't like setting her brother up, and who could blame her? She had a right to see how everything turned out. Besides, if he didn't plan for her presence, she'd still come, putting herself and the whole operation in danger. "Very well. I'll show you where to wait."

She opened her mouth to protest but had the good sense not to speak. If he thought she would put herself in danger, he might lock her in a cell for the night. "Where?"

His mind raced. The convoy would approach the bridge from Burlington to the south. The robbers might hole up on either side of the bridge, or even underneath. He led her to the far end. "The best place is going to be that stand of trees." He nodded toward a spot at the corner of his cousin's property.

She nudged her horse forward, and he followed until they were both beneath the evergreen boughs. Swinging the mare around, she peered through the dense branches. "I can't see anything from here." She trotted the horse forward until only the tail ends of the branches stood between her and the clearing. "I can see a little bit from here, but not much."

The problem was that they could see her as well. Once again he wished he could lock her in a jail cell until the excitement was over.

She sat back in the saddle and looked at him over her shoulder. "Your men won't be waiting here. It's too far away to help if something goes wrong."

Even before she opened her mouth, he knew what she would say. "I want to be with them." She must have seen the hesitation in his face. "I insist. I have a right. If I'm. . . betraying—" At the word, her voice broke, but her back remained ramrod straight. "If Lewis is involved, I want to see it for myself."

Daniel's admiration for Clara grew in proportion to his frustration. This maddening woman refused to stay behind the sidelines. She didn't close her eyes to what was wrong with the world, but rather sought to change it. He couldn't change her mind any more than he could change himself. He didn't know that he wanted to.

"A sentinel will be up there." He pointed to a small hilltop a short distance away, almost indistinguishable from the forest around it. "He can see the road as well as much of the surrounding countryside. He'll know when someone approaches the bridge."

"What if they come early?"

"He'll be in place before dawn. In fact, he's spending the night up there." He smiled grimly. "It's my brother Hiram. There's no one better than he at this kind of thing. He climbs up there when he's hunting for deer and always comes home with meat."

"And the others?"

"The men driving the wagon—young Dixon and a few men from Burlington—will circle back after they hand the money bags over to me."

"Money bags? Surely you're not carrying actual currency." Her gray eyes had retreated behind her glasses and the hood of her cloak, to where all he could see was a dark gleam.

"No, but the bags will look full. They have to believe we have money." He and Simeon had spent a couple of hours weighing out stones equivalent to a shipment of gold coin.

"Will you have someone waiting at the bridge?" She broke the edge of the trees and returned to the open, her eyes scanning the empty farm fields. A lone eagle hovered overhead.

Daniel stared at her a long moment. "You're not going to give up, are you?"

She shook her head and urged her horse to move ahead. "I don't much know about such things, but I haven't seen anything that would provide good cover."

"How much do you know of the Tuttle family history?" He came beside her.

"Enough. You told us a lot on Thursday."

"I didn't mention this part. Come this way" He left the

road and guided them through a narrow stand of trees. "They'll be waiting here. At the Reids' cave." He brought the horses to a halt in front of an opening low enough that both of them would have to stoop to enter.

❧

"Of course." Memories washed over Clara, tales so tall she never quite knew if she believed them, stories of the Reid family living in a cave during the War for Independence.

"Yes, it's all true. At least most of it is." Daniel smiled and offered her his hand. "I was about to say the bank is too steep, but if my great-grandmother managed it when she was in a family way, I'm sure you'll be fine. Just watch your footing."

Clara bent over and peered into the dark recess. "I can't see anything."

"Let me." He took her place at the opening and felt around inside, coming up with a candle. He lit it and, bending down, entered the cave. She followed behind.

The cave smelled dank and musty, as if no air blew through to an exit on the other side. Stones marked an old fire pit in the center. A mouse whisked away in the shadows, hiding in the spout of an old coffeepot. For some reason, she didn't mind his presence here. Mice belonged in underground places. She only hoped she would never have to share their living quarters.

"Look out the entrance." Daniel interrupted her inspection.

She stuck her head out the opening and let the fresh air caress her face. He stooped down beside her. "There's the bridge." He pointed up and to the left. "We can see people entering the bridge from either end or even someone hiding underneath."

Clara could almost imagine shadows dancing on the rocks

beneath the bridge, and she fought a temptation to pull back. She had nothing to fear on a sunny afternoon. "Can you see the cave from the bridge?"

She felt more than saw him shake his head. "Not unless you know where to look. Or unless someone lights the candle." She heard his hiss of breath, and the candle sputtered out. "Which they won't tomorrow."

A man on horseback approached the bridge from the side heading into town. Pastor Beaton carried a rifle swung over his back and a pack on the horse, probably filled with his Bible and other things that would bring solace to the more far-flung families of his parish. He had been an army chaplain in his earlier life, spending ten years in the military, including service in Mexico, before he became their pastor.

The horse's hooves alerted them to his passage across the bridge. He paused on their side of the bridge, only a few feet away from their hiding place, and dropped the toll in the waiting box. They could see the underbelly of the horse, the slightly worn leather of the girth that needed to be replaced, but the pastor appeared to have no knowledge of their presence. Clara followed his passage until he disappeared a few yards past the bridge.

"Satisfied?" Daniel grinned.

"When do I need to be here?"

thirteen

Lewis dashed Clara's last hopes of escaping oncoming events when he left home before dinner on Friday night, telling her not to wait for him. When she arose early in the morning— so early some might call it a late night instead—he hadn't returned to his room. He had taken the bait.

During the few minutes it took her to assemble food for breakfast and lunch, she hoped Lewis would breeze in, even if he stank like a drunk skunk. If he came back, she might tell him the gold shipment was a trap, that he should stay as far away from the bridge as possible.

She shivered, the kitchen cold without the heat of the stove, and wondered if she could keep up the pretense.

In the end, her hesitation hadn't mattered. Lewis hadn't come home. She dressed in breeches—not wanting to give any passersby reason to wonder why a woman would wander alone outside at that time of night—tucked a pistol into the waistband, and left the house as the moon started to set.

Daniel hadn't wanted her to walk so far, but what choice did she have? If Lewis spotted Misty at the bridge, he would suspect trouble. Even if she left the mare in town, Lewis might still be suspicious. No, she would do better to arrive on foot and leave Misty at home. She had plenty of time. In the cool reaches of the night, she practiced the swagger that men seemed to use when walking. What had Daniel said once? "You're all woman, from the pretty curls on top of your head to your tiny feet." Her face burned with the memory, and she felt under the brim of her cap for her curls. None had escaped, at least not yet, and no one could see the size of her feet in the dark. So perhaps she could pass for a male.

The sky had changed to a shade lighter than black by the time she reached town. A dark figure approached her out of the shadows, and she jumped.

"It's me." A deep voice she recognized as Daniel's reassured her. He drew near and pulled back his cap, revealing the banked embers of his eyes in the pale light of his face. He fell into step beside her. "I would tuck my arm beneath yours, but people might wonder why I was walking arm in arm with another man." She felt a ripple of silent laughter pass down his side. "You didn't fool me, though."

"You knew I was headed this way."

"True. Do you want some coffee? I have some on the stove in the jail. Fresh made, so it's not undrinkable yet."

She glanced at the still, dark sky and gauged she had some time to spare. But staying in the light and warmth of the jail only delayed the inevitable. "My nerves are already frayed. I don't need something else to make it worse. Another time." *When I'm visiting my brother in jail.* "Have any plans changed since yesterday?"

"Nothing you need to know about." He stopped beneath a tree at the southwest corner of the common. "Go as far as the bridge. Brent Frisk will meet you there." He gripped her left arm with his right. "Do you want to call the whole plan off? We can, even now." Shoulders rigid with tension, he looked as though he might crack apart into a dozen separate pieces, and his fingers bit into her skin.

Tears sprang to her eyes, but not from the pain. "No. Lewis

must accept responsibility for his actions."

"I wish. . ." He cleared his throat. "I wish things didn't have to be this way."

He released her, and she caught hold of him instead. "I do, as well. I wish you didn't have to put yourself in harm's way because of my brother's actions."

She stared into his eyes, and in an instant they blazed from banked coals to a raging fire. He pulled her to himself in a tight embrace, kissed her briefly on the lips, and released her. "Go."

The cry rent her heart.

&

Daniel waited beneath the tree until even the smudge of Clara's shadow disappeared in the distance. He wanted to run after her. To at least sit with her in the dark cave, to keep her company and comfort her as she waited for the inevitable. But he had a different role to play in the day's events.

I wish you didn't have to put yourself in harm's way. Oh, Clara, if she only knew. He would stand between her and death and pour out his lifeblood, if need be. Due to a last-minute change of plans, however, he didn't anticipate any true danger today.

At length he shook himself out of his reverie. If anyone caught sight of him lingering at the corner of the green, staring down the road when the moon had fallen and no light existed to see by, they would wonder about the object of his thoughts. Across the common, footsteps scurried down the street, probably Fannie on her way to the café to begin the day's baking. In another hour, he might be able to convince her to serve him a cup of her ridiculous coffee and a hot-from-the-oven cinnamon bun before riding out to keep his appointment with doom at the bridge.

Daniel hadn't done more than doze last night, so he should have felt exhausted, but his eyes stayed open as they had before many a battle. No amount of counting sheep jumping over fences had put him to sleep. A short nap might refresh him, if he could manage it. He unlocked one of the cells and stretched out on the thin mattress. In the corner, he heard a scuffling and half expected a mouse to crawl up his leg. A smile lifted his lips at the memory of Clara's fear of the mouse on the bridge. Not long ago, Hiram's cat had had a litter of kittens. He'd grab one of them as a mouser.

Something creaked, and he bolted upright, staring into the inky blackness of the office. "Who's there?" Grabbing his revolver, he ran to his office, only to feel a breeze pushing past cracks in the door.

He went back to the cell but gave up on sleep. Bending over, he found the tiny hole where the mouse had disappeared at the approach of the big human ogre. Could anything fill up the hole so a small creature couldn't crawl through? The floor could use a thorough sweeping. Lye soap and bleach might be needed to soak the smells out of the walls.

At last he judged enough time had passed that he could pretend it was the start of an ordinary day. First off, he'd make a quick stop at the house to shave the whiskers from his cheeks and change clothes into something unremarkable.

Half an hour later, when the grandfather clock in the parlor announced five o'clock of the morning, he left the house as refreshed as clean clothes and cold water could make him. By this hour, he could squeak into the café. He needed to be around people before he set out on his quest for his imagined opponent, a dark, evil shadow who wanted to haunt his dreams at night. Something of even less substance than the mouse and her babies.

A single lamp on the front table in the café provided all the light for the dining room that morning. Light gleamed from the kitchen. "Fannie?"

She came out, still wearing an apron dotted with flour. Not everyone knew that Fannie baked all the pastries for the café herself, although she depended on a cook for meals. "You're early." She wiped her hands on the apron before removing it and hanging it on a peg. "Let me light more lamps."

"I'll just take a cup of coffee and a cinnamon roll. I've got to get going." He settled down by the front table, where the one lamp provided sufficient light. Fannie poured him a cup of coffee and bustled into the kitchen. She returned a few minutes later with the requested roll and a slice of ham, quickly browned. "It isn't much, but a man needs more than a sweet roll to keep him going."

Daniel let the roll melt in his mouth and chewed down the ham between swallows of the coffee. From his seat, he saw Simeon passing by and longed to call him in. Daniel could imagine Fannie's reaction if that happened.

Mr. Tuttle! I suppose you want to join your brother? And what brings the two of you out so early this morning? Knowing Fannie, she would pass on the news to all of her customers.

No, that wouldn't do at all. In a few hours' time, the whole town might buzz with the coming affair at the bridge, but until then, Daniel needed to stick as closely as possible to his usual schedule. He finished the meal a tad more quickly than usual and left money on the table. "Keep the change." He headed out the door.

The sky had moved from pale gray to pale blue shot with brilliant pinks and yellows in the east. He returned to the jail. One last time, he checked that his pistol was loaded and ready for action. His saddle was fixed to receive the money bags. He climbed onto his horse. The gelding sensed his direction, for before Daniel even flicked his reins, he'd turned his nose in the direction of the bridge. When Daniel's shift of the rein confirmed the direction, he set off at a trot. The temperature this morning was about ten degrees higher than yesterday morning; no frost hardened the ground, and the ride went as quietly as it could with four hooves hitting the ground at regular intervals.

Daniel's nerves itched to give Spotty his head and let him gallop, but the horse might need his wind later. Besides, if he hurried, he might arrive at the bridge too early. At most, he wanted to arrive half an hour before the carriage from Burlington. They had planned to leave before daylight to make the rendezvous.

When Daniel reached the bridge, he dismounted, casually scanning the area for signs of another presence. He led Spotty to the side of the road and tethered him to a tree. Daylight caught him pacing back and forth like an army sentry in front of the east entrance to the bridge. From there, the men waiting in the cave could see him, as well as anyone in or under the bridge. The last rays of the rising sun might distort their vision for a few vital seconds, long enough to give him an advantage.

Fifteen minutes remained, twenty at most. Every drop of coffee he'd drunk over the past twenty-four hours stretched his eyesight. He felt like he could see to the depths of the earth and all the way to California, but in reality he couldn't even see the cave on the far side of the river.

He hoped that didn't prove a fatal error.

❧

Clara counted Daniel's steps as he paced back and forth. Forward march, ten steps. About face. Ten steps return. Each step as carefully measured as if his feet knew the width of the bridge and could pace it blindfolded. Something about his determined pace troubled her.

"Miss Farley." Frisk, one of Daniel's deputies, tapped her on the shoulder. "I need to change places with you."

She stepped back. How foolish of her, staring like a spectator when the men in the cave with her needed to watch for Daniel's safety.

Daniel's safety. "He's setting himself up as a target." She wanted to scream, to run out of the cave and tell him to go away.

"Stay still, ma'am. We won't let anything happen to the captain."

The ground overhead trembled, suggesting the approach of the carriage. Several stones tumbled down the slope and crashed into the water, and Clara leaned past Frisk far enough to see half a dozen men crawl from beneath the bridge.

Rifle shots rang out. When the smoke cleared, Daniel had disappeared from view.

fourteen

Clara jolted to her feet, poised to dash out the entrance.

The carriage, with Dixon and two other men she didn't recognize, continued full speed onto the bridge.

The men from the cave raced to join them. Only Frisk paused long enough to yell. "Stay in the cave! Captain's orders."

I won't stay behind. I'm not defenseless. She grabbed the pistol she had tucked in the waistband of her breeches. Her racing heart jumped ahead of her onto the road, but she forced herself to check her surroundings. All the action remained at the far side of the bridge, and she dashed forward.

She took a second at the entrance to the bridge to let her eyes adjust to the semi-darkness of the interior. The reverberating echoes sounded like she imagined an earthquake would, the monstrous noise threatening to tear down the bridge and everyone on it. Horses' hooves pounded on the planks like sledgehammers. A dozen men's voices snarled together, a black cloud of incomprehensible noise. Her mind catalogued the sounds. She heard more pounding of fists and shouts than gunfire and took small comfort in that. After her eyes had adjusted, she crept forward. "That does it!"

Daniel had his good arm around the neck of one of the assailants, dressed in the same hat and bandanna she had seen at the bank.

"You think you have it easy because you're dealing with a crippled man?"

Clara hardly recognized the raspy voice as Daniel's.

"You think you can have your way in *my* town!" He yanked his arm so hard that the man flailed for breath.

The handkerchief slid down from his nose under the pressure of Daniel's arm, and Clara recognized the face of one of the Whitson twins—Rod, she believed. Where Whitson was, Lewis would not be far behind, but none of the figures in front of her reminded her of her brother.

"I've got him." Dixon appeared at Daniel's side and tied Whitson's hands together. Daniel gave his neck a final tug before he let him go.

They tied each man's hands together and then tied the robbers to each other. Daniel walked by and whisked the hats off their heads. "The Whitson twins. Whimsey, Bradford, Dupre, Ford." He spit out each name. "Not a one of you is missing."

No one except, that is, for—Lewis.

"Surprised?" A low voice spoke in her ear, and she screamed. All the men froze in place for so long that the robbers could have escaped if they weren't already bound.

"Clara!" Daniel's voice, half exultant, half exasperated, boomed and echoed through the bridge chamber. "I thought I told you to stay in the cave."

"You were in danger." Her voice quavered. "The shots. . ." She realized how silly she sounded, as if she, a lone woman, could protect him if all his accomplices had failed.

"I was never in any danger." Daniel's eyes blazed in the dark, and he crossed the space between them in a few easy strides. "Not with Lewis on my side." He draped his arm over Lewis's shoulders.

"I have a lot to tell you." Lewis said, low enough so that only she and Daniel could hear.

"What happened?" She stared at the two men, one of whom she had loved since childhood, the other who had become dear to her over the past few weeks. She wanted to bang their heads together for letting her worry so, about *both* of them.

❧

Daniel shut the door on his protesting prisoners and turned the key until the lock clicked into place. "Fannie will bring you supper. It's too late for lunch." She would have brought food—if only to hear the news firsthand—but he wanted them to squirm a little bit. He turned to his deputy. "You sure you don't mind staying?"

Dixon sat behind the desk, feet planted on the ground. Daniel felt sure that his face mirrored the foolish grin on his friend's. The accused robbers would stay in the Maple Notch jail until they were taken to the county seat for trial. Until that day came, Daniel and Dixon would take turns guarding them. "Go on with you. Get down to that girl of yours before she decides you're not coming."

Daniel laughed as he hadn't in years. On his way out the door, he reached for his forage cap where it hung on its peg, then dropped his hand. The time had come to put Captain Tuttle behind him. Daniel was more than ready to be a civilian lawman. He had grown into the name of Constable Tuttle.

He found Lewis and Clara in the café. They must have gone home, because Clara had exchanged her breeches for a lavender gingham dress. Her face shone with greater color than usual, her excitement at the morning's events evident in her features. He joined them at the table.

"I ordered for all of us. I hope you don't mind."

"Good idea. So, Lewis, have you told Clara our plans for this afternoon?"

He shook his head. "I was waiting for you."

Clara punched her brother in the arm. "He hasn't told me *anything*, only that I would have to wait for you." The smile on her face faded. "Lewis, you knew I suspected you."

"And you were right." Lewis screwed his face into tight lines. "I did take part in the first robbery, helped them gain entrance for the second, and gave them information about today's shipment."

The look Clara threw Daniel's way let him know she wondered if her brother should be confessing all of this in front of the constable. She didn't know he had already heard the whole story.

Fannie arrived with the sandwiches—thick slices of roast beef with mustard on fine wheat bread, with a side dish of potato salad. Daniel knew she wanted to learn the news. "Give us a few minutes, Fannie. I'll tell you all about it later."

A mutinous look on her face let him know *later* wouldn't be as satisfying as *now*, but she nodded. "I'll bring you out a pitcher so you can refill your own glasses, and then I'll leave you alone."

The lunch hour had passed, and with Fannie's departure, they had privacy. Daniel decided to put Clara's worries to rest. "Lewis came to me late last night. Told me about their plan to rob the shipment today at the bridge and offered to help me stop them."

"Wasn't I surprised when he told me they *wanted* us to make the attempt, but I could help." Lewis's part involved making sure the guns had no ammunition or would misfire. He also promised to warn Daniel of their approach.

"The rocks hitting the water," she remembered.

"We wanted to catch them red-handed, you see."

The shots Clara had heard had come from Daniel, fired as a warning. Unbeknownst to her, Daniel had additional men waiting on the town side of the bridge, ready to come to his rescue.

"So between the men in the cave and the men on the carriage and the men with me, we outnumbered them two to one. It wasn't even a fair battle." Daniel grinned. "I like those kinds of odds."

"And this afternoon?" Clara took a bite of pumpkin pie, and a bit of whipped cream landed at the side of her lip. She licked it off, and Daniel's tongue thickened too much for him to speak.

"I'm going to show you where we hid the money." Lewis picked at his pie. "What's left of it, that is." His shoulders collapsed in on themselves, like a piece of paper folded in half.

Act like a man, Daniel chided him silently.

Lewis unfolded his shoulders and put his hands palms down on the table, his eyes fixing Daniel to his seat. "I will make what restitution I can. I'll work for the rest. If anyone will hire me, that is, after what I've done."

Daniel looked to Clara. Would she offer to make up the difference? Tears glinted behind her glasses, but she didn't speak.

"I'm sure the judge will take your cooperation into consideration when it comes to sentencing."

A single tear escaped Clara's left eye and slid down her

cheek. He longed to reach out with his hand and brush it away, but he held himself back.

"Sentencing?" Confusion clouded Clara's face. "But you didn't arrest him."

Daniel looked around, not wanting the slightest whisper of this conversation to reach Fannie's ears. But before he spoke, Lewis answered. "He told me I was under arrest when I went to him this morning. I don't have to stay in jail, however, as long as I show up at court on time."

Clara turned her mourning dove eyes on Daniel. "You took a big risk."

Uncomfortable with her appreciation, he shrugged. "I figured it was worth taking a chance on someone who came forward like that." He took the last bite of pie. "Are we ready to go?"

❧

The horses worked their way through dense trees to a spot far southeast of town, not far from Whitson's farm. Branches tore at Clara's face and dress, making her wish she still wore the britches. She only hoped all the rents could be repaired.

Whatever tears the brambles created in her clothing could be more easily repaired than the rents to her heart. Her worst fears about Lewis's involvement had been confirmed, yet transformed somehow by his offer to help Daniel. Why hadn't either one of them told her?

"It's there." Lewis pointed to a gigantic oak that must have been standing before Columbus discovered America. As they approached, she could see the tree was dying from rot from the inside out, dry limbs caught in the lace of the upper branches, the roots pulling loose from the earth.

Daniel dismounted and helped her down before grabbing

the shovel from the back of his horse. He handed the tool to Lewis. "Dig."

Instead, Lewis dropped to the ground and pushed aside a pile of damp leaves sitting between two of the biggest roots. The ground he exposed had been recently disturbed. With a few shovelfuls of dirt, the edge of a burlap sack emerged. She held her breath.

He tugged out two bags and set them on the ground before digging deeper with the shovel. This time he exposed a canvas sack almost sunshine bright in its newness. He dug all the dirt around it, and then used both arms to lift it out. Clara guessed that bag held the gold coins.

After he placed all three sacks at Daniel's feet like a penitent's offering, Lewis took a step back and crossed his arms behind him. Trying to present an unthreatening appearance, she supposed.

"Is that it?" Daniel asked.

Lewis nodded. "We spent a chunk of the bills on that weekend drunk. When we grabbed the gold coins, we realized we couldn't spend it without drawing attention to ourselves, so we decided to each take a little but to leave most of it here and decide how to divide it later." A pale pink dusted his cheeks.

Daniel muttered something that sounded like "honor among thieves."

"I can't be sure, but I don't think anyone has disturbed it since we buried it."

When Daniel opened the burlap sacks, paper money and coins spilled out. Neat stacks of ones and fives, tens and twenties were banded together. He thumbed through them, counting swiftly. "Missing about fifty dollars from what Simeon told me."

"That sounds about right." Lewis pointed to his feet, encased in a new pair of Congress boots. "Want my boots? I bought them with some of that money."

Daniel growled, and Clara moved to her brother's side. She put her hand on his shoulder, a small, comforting gesture like their mother used to offer. "And the gold coins?"

"The bag is plenty heavy. But I'll have to wait until we get back to town to count it out and verify the amounts." Daniel let a few coins slip through his fingers. "Recovering this means a lot. I'm pretty sure Simeon will speak on your behalf to the judge."

"Restitution. It's the right thing to do, and doesn't the Bible say something about paying back more than what you took?" Lewis grimaced. "I guess the court will determine how much."

Daniel hefted the three bags with his single arm as if they weighed no more than a straw tick and secured them in his saddlebags. "Let's go, then." Instead of returning the way they had come, he moved forward. "I'm pretty sure we're close to Whitson's farm from here. I want to check on how Baruch is faring." He paused. "And make sure Mr. Whitson has heard about the twins."

Clara doubted their welcome, but she mounted her horse. After a moment's hesitation, Lewis joined them. They let the silence of the forest envelop them.

"The house is just through those trees." Lewis nodded and trotted his horse straight ahead.

A shot rang out, and Lewis screamed.

❧

Daniel burst through the trees in two seconds. Lewis lay on the ground, blood streaming from his shoulder.

"Stay away from me and mine." Old Whitson waited on the porch, his feet spread far apart, rifle held against his shoulder.

"Mr. Whitson, it's me, Daniel Tuttle, the constable." His hand wanted to reach for the comfort of his pistol, but he resisted. He took a step forward.

"Don't move." Whitson shook his rifle. "You Tuttles have always been trouble. Now you've got my boys in jail."

Daniel didn't think Whitson would appreciate a reminder that his sons had robbed the bank and brought it on themselves. He stayed still. "I'm right sorry about that."

Whitson snorted.

Daniel moved a step closer. He caught a glimpse of something out of the corner of his eyes. "How is Baruch faring?" He dipped his chin, and Baruch moved into place behind his father.

With a single movement, Baruch removed the rifle from his father's grasp. "I'm doing much better, thanks for asking." His expression didn't offer much more welcome than his father's had, but he took in the heavy saddle bags on the back of Daniel's horse. "So it's true. My brothers robbed the bank."

Daniel felt movement behind him. Lewis had pulled himself to his feet and took his place at his side. "They did, with some help. Including mine."

"So you caught the shot." Whitson glared at Lewis. "Too bad I just winged you."

"I'll be all right."

The four men faced off, none of them willing to move, claims and counterclaims roiling through the air. Again Daniel sensed movement, and Clara slipped past him to stand between the opposing sides.

"Mr. Whitson." Looking as harmless as a dove on her nest, Clara smiled as if this was an ordinary social call. "I wanted to tell you how much I enjoyed having Libby in my class this week. She told such wonderful stories of how your family fought in the War for Independence." She waved her hands as if indicating the strands of the story and moved forward. "And now your son Baruch has proved just as brave. Something more to add to the lore of Maple Notch."

Some of the vinegar went out of Whitson's face. "That's true. She's a real cracker. And I've always been proud of Baruch."

Clara had defused a sour situation by the simple expedient of reminding Whitson of two children who gave him cause for pride. She'd make a fine teacher—no doubt about it—or even a politician. Daniel's lips curled at the thought. She'd argue that women should be able to hold public office, if they wanted to.

"I reckon I'd like Libby to go to that fancy school of yours, if you ever get it started."

"And I'd be honored to have her." Clara closed the distance between them and shook his hand, as grimy and smelly as he must be.

With a sister like that, Lewis was bound to turn things around. She wouldn't give him any choice.

When Clara cocked her head in his direction, Daniel felt the full force of her smile. Now that he had nabbed the robbers, he would let her know she had no choice, none at all, when it came to a husband.

epilogue

After Christmas, when winter held Maple Notch in its grasp, most people stayed at home if they had a choice, but not Clara. Too much had happened since the raid on St. Albans for her to take the time off.

The robbers had been taken to Hyde Park to await trial. Lewis remained free, although he would stand trial with the others. His lawyer held hopes that he would receive a reduced sentence for his role in capturing the gang and returning the money. Lewis wasn't asking for any special treatment. He said he had disobeyed the law of God and the law of the land and deserved punishment. Those words alone made Clara want to weep. Aside from those tears, she was happier than she had been for a long time.

Between Lewis's problems and Christmas festivities, Clara had to rush to prepare the Bailey Mansion for the first class of the Maple Notch Seminary for Females. Two of the older girls from the local school would join two boarders sent her way by her mentor, Miss Featherton, on the first of February. Daniel had proved easy to work with. His suggestions for her plans proved sensible in most cases; she'd had to argue her point on a few others.

Daniel. He was the main reason she couldn't stop smiling and didn't feel the cold, even when snow fell like it did today. Since the confrontation at Whitson's farm, he had spent every spare minute with her. She told herself it was only because they had to conclude the business about the house, nothing more.

Her traitorous heart didn't always agree, however, reminding her of the time he had kissed the top of her head, or the tender way he looked at her when he thought she wouldn't notice as they explored his grandparents' house.

"You're looking fine."

At the sound of Lewis's deep voice, Clara whirled around, causing her skirt to swish in a wide circle. She had fashioned two new dresses with wider skirts, still avoiding the ridiculous hoops. They swirled in unexpected directions when she turned abruptly, but oh, they made her feel so feminine.

"Don't forget these." He reached for the ermine muff he had given her for Christmas. "They're perfect with your coat." He removed the red cloak from the coat tree and draped it over her shoulders. "Have fun today."

Someone knocked, and Lewis opened the door to Daniel. Fashionable ladies might make him wait, but not Clara. She saw the sleigh on the road in front of her house, and she giggled like a schoolgirl. What could be better than a sleigh ride in the twilight of a winter snowfall with a man—especially this man?

"I take it you are ready." Daniel bowed deeply. The dark blue overcoat looked magnificent on his manly figure. He went bareheaded, and his ears looked red.

"Your head," Clara said. "You'll catch cold."

"I have a hat on the sleigh. But I don't care for knitted caps." He shook his head, and some of his hair fell over his ears. "That's why God gave us hair, after all."

They said good-bye to Lewis. Clara slipped as she minced her way across the icy expanse of her yard, but Daniel held her tight, a solid, sturdy man. No one he cared for would ever come to harm.

He helped her into her seat and tucked a blanket around her. "And here's a warming brick for your feet." He put something warm underneath her boots. A moment later, he joined her on the sleigh.

A matched pair of white horses, almost as white as the falling snow, pulled the sleigh, and the bells on their harness jingled as they trotted down the road. The runners glided over the icy surface that had proved so hazardous to her feet. They skimmed down the road as easily as a duck swimming in water. The snow lent an air of newness to everything around them.

They reached the town green in a matter of minutes. Pastor Beaton came out of the church. "Beautiful day for a sleigh ride, isn't it?"

Daniel saluted him without answering. His ears had turned so red Clara feared they might suffer frostbite. She wiggled her left hand out of her muff and reached for the nearest ear, rubbing it between thumb and forefinger.

Daniel jerked. "Watch out! That tickles!"

She laughed. "Then wear your hat." Without waiting for his answer, she took the knitted cap she found on the seat and pulled it over the crown of his head until it covered his ears.

He took them around the common twice, each turn of the sleigh causing her to slide a little closer to him. The third time around, he headed the horses down Bridge Road. "I helped Hiram roll snow across the bridge yesterday." He wiggled his eyebrows, which snow crystals had turned to a hoary white. "I'm warning you, I'll take off my hat as soon as we stop."

She laughed. "Why are we stopping on the bridge?" *It is called The Courting Bridge.* Did she dare hope?

He turned his gaze on her, something unreadable in his eyes. "You'll see."

A few minutes later, the bridge came into view. The falling snow had turned it into a winter fairytale, a place wondrous enough for the Eskimos she'd read about in faraway Alaska. She wished she could capture the bright red walls, the white snow mounded on the roof like a European castle, in paint.

Daniel slowed the horses, and they plodded onto the bridge. *They call them kissing bridges, because if you drive the team slow enough, a fellow can kiss a girl twice before you get across.* That bit of folklore jumped into Clara's mind, and she felt her cheeks heat, probably turning as red as Daniel's ears.

But Daniel made no move to kiss her and, in fact, let the horses come to a complete standstill in the middle of the bridge. "Remember where we are?" White teeth showed between his dark mustache and beard, grown over the winter months. He tugged the hat off his head.

She resisted the obvious—Tuttle Bridge—and looked around her. To her left, a few feet from where Daniel held the reins to the horses, she saw a scarred wooden plank. Her heartbeat sped.

He seemed to sense the moment she recognized the spot, jumping down before helping her out of the sleigh. He clasped one of her hands in his and walked with her to the plank. Once there, he let go of her hand to pull a knife from his pocket. "I think it's time we add our own bit to Maple Notch history." He nodded at the plank. "If you're willing?"

One look in his eyes told her that her traitorous heart had guessed right, after all. "As long as we do it together."

"I wouldn't dream of doing it any other way. How about—right there?" He found a blank spot to the right of his parents' initials.

She placed her right hand over his larger one and felt him draw the knife down in a solid stroke, the left side of the *D. T* soon followed, then the plus sign. He lifted his hand away and placed the knife in her palm. "Do you want to finish?"

Now his hand covered hers as her fingers drew the uncertain curve of the *C* and then an *F* into the wood. She closed the knife but didn't move. Instead she leaned back into the breadth of Daniel's chest.

"Clara." His voice caressed her name. "After the war, I never thought God would have a woman for me."

She shifted, wanting to turn, to look him in the face, but he held her firmly in place.

"But then I met you again. I ran into you everywhere I turned, it seemed. It didn't take long for this stubborn fool to realize I loved you more than anything in life, except for my Lord and Savior." His shoulders shook, but his voice held firm. "I'm not much of a catch. I'm missing half an arm, and I don't know if I want to be constable of Maple Notch for all my life or where else God might lead me. But there is no one who will love you more. Tell me, Clara, are you willing to join your life with mine as we have joined our initials?"

This time when she turned in his arms, he didn't stop her. She brought her hand to where it rested on the stump of Daniel's left elbow. "This"—she increased the pressure ever so slightly—"makes no difference to me. You are more of a man than anyone else I know. As long as you don't mind an old maid who wears glasses."

"I hope her students—and her daughters—grow up to

be just like her." He touched her cheek with the back of his hand. "Is that a yes?"

She looked into his hazel eyes, fiery now with need and desire. Daniel freed her hair from its hairnet, running his fingers through the long tresses. "I love you, Clara Farley." He shouted it at the top of his lungs.

"Oh, Daniel." She traced her finger over his beard. "I love you, too."

Their lips joined in a kiss sweet enough to last a lifetime.

A Letter To Our Readers

Dear Reader:

In order that we might better contribute to your reading enjoyment, we would appreciate your taking a few minutes to respond to the following questions. We welcome your comments and read each form and letter we receive. When completed, please return to the following:

Fiction Editor
Heartsong Presents
PO Box 719
Uhrichsville, Ohio 44683

1. Did you enjoy reading *Love's Raid* by Darlene Franklin?
   ❑ Very much! I would like to see more books by this author!
   ❑ Moderately. I would have enjoyed it more if

   _____

   _____

   _____

2. Are you a member of **Heartsong Presents**? ❑ Yes ❑ No
   If no, where did you purchase this book? _____

   _____

3. How would you rate, on a scale from 1 (poor) to 5 (superior), the cover design? _____

4. On a scale from 1 (poor) to 10 (superior), please rate the following elements.

   ____ Heroine   ____ Plot
   ____ Hero   ____ Inspirational theme
   ____ Setting   ____ Secondary characters

5. These characters were special because? _____

_____

_____

6. How has this book inspired your life?_____

_____

_____

7. What settings would you like to see covered in future
   Heartsong Presents books? _____

_____

_____

8. What are some inspirational themes you would like to see
   treated in future books? _____

_____

_____

9. Would you be interested in reading other **Heartsong
   Presents** titles? ☐ Yes ☐ No

10. Please check your age range:
    ☐ Under 18   ☐ 18-24
    ☐ 25-34   ☐ 35-45
    ☐ 46-55   ☐ Over 55

Name _____

Occupation _____

Address _____

City, State, Zip_____

E-mail _____

RUGGED & RELENTLESS

Jacob Granger is chasing down his brother's murderer. His only clue?—a circled and most unusual ad that leads him to Hopefalls where he cashes in on his logging experience and pretends to court Evelyn Thompson. Will this feller find himself falling for the entrepreneurial female and foregoing his lust for vengeance?

Historical, paperback, 320 pages, 5.5" x 8.375"

_____

HEARTSONG
PRESENTS

If you love Christian romance...

$12.⁹⁹

You'll love Heartsong Presents' inspiring and faith-filled romances by today's very best Christian authors...Wanda E. Brunstetter, Mary Connealy, Susan Page Davis, Cathy Marie Hake, and Joyce Livingston, to mention a few!

When you join Heartsong Presents, you'll enjoy four brand-new, mass-market, 176-page books—two contemporary and two historical—that will build you up in your faith when you discover God's role in every relationship you read about!

Mass Market 176 Pages

Imagine...four new romances every four weeks—with men and women like you who long to meet the one God has chosen as the love of their lives...all for the low price of $12.99 postpaid.

To join, simply visit www.heartsong presents.com or complete the coupon below and mail it to the address provided.

YES! Sign me up for Heartso❤ng!

NEW MEMBERSHIPS WILL BE SHIPPED IMMEDIATELY!
Send no money now. We'll bill you only $12.99 postpaid with your first shipment of four books. Or for faster action, call 1-740-922-7280.

NAME _____

ADDRESS_____

CITY_____ STATE _____ ZIP _____

MAIL TO: HEARTSONG PRESENTS, P.O. Box 721, Uhrichsville, Ohio 44683
or sign up at WWW.HEARTSONGPRESENTS.COM